THE
COLLECTED
WORKS
OF
MAVIS
HOPGOOD

The story "Utah Died for your Sins" was initially published in *Quarry West* and was subsequently awarded and anthologized in *The Pushcart Prize.*

The poems "After You Set Your Head on Fire" and "Newly Wed" originally appeared in *Painted Bride Quarterly.*

The story "The China Doll" was originally published in *Another Chicago Magazine.*

The anecdote "Jimmy" originally appeared in *Kit Car Builder Magazine* and was subsequently anthologized in the book *Actual Mileage.*

The work contained in this collection is otherwise new. With the exception of the foregoing, no poem, story, or anecdote contained herein has been submitted elsewhere for publication.

A Stormy Weather Book

Cover and interior design by David J. High, highdzn.com.
Interior composition by Ken Hansen.

ISBN 978-0-9997975-4-9

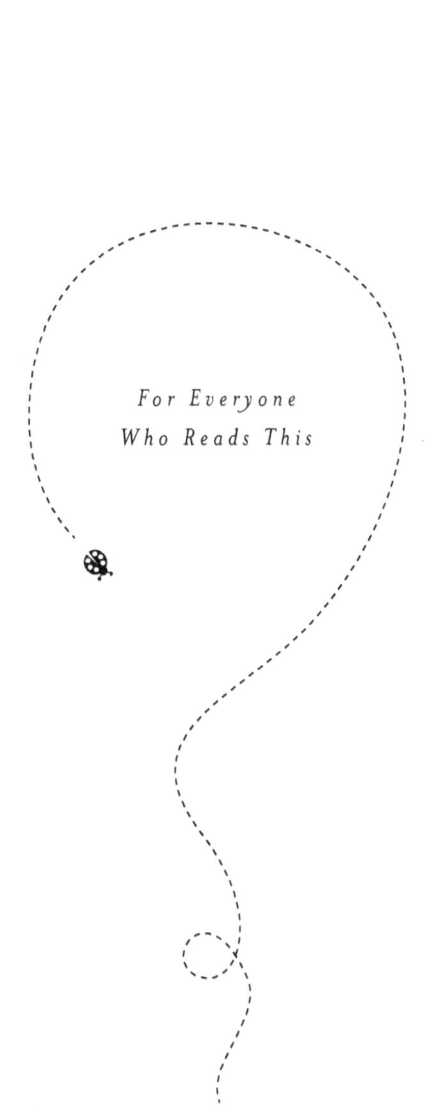

For Everyone
Who Reads This

THE COLLECTED WORKS OF MAVIS HOPGOOD

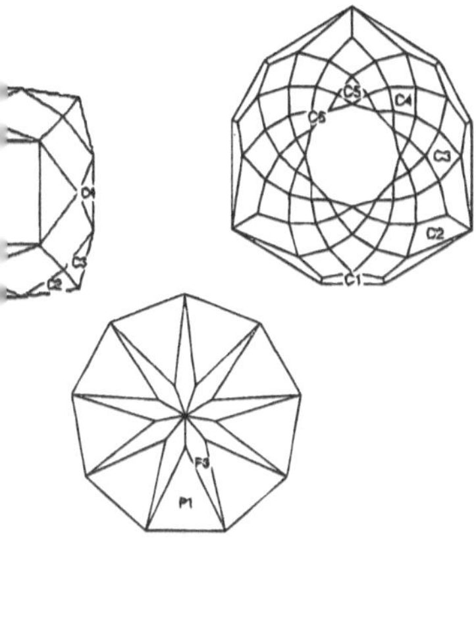

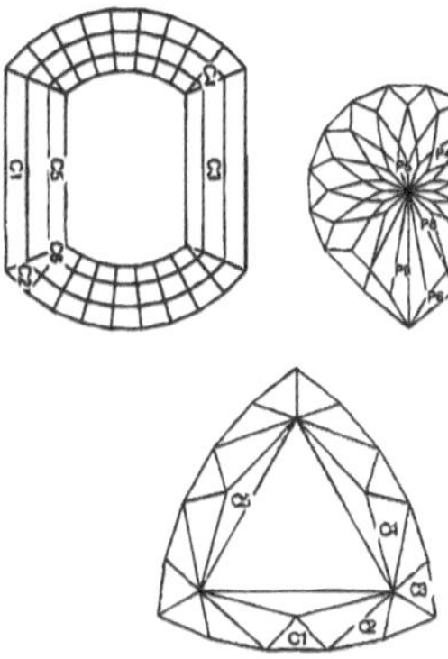

MAX ZIMMER

STORMY WEATHER Publishing

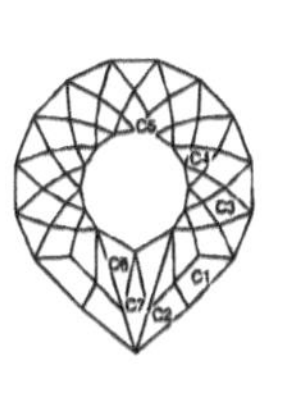

C5
C4
C3
C6
C1
C7
C2

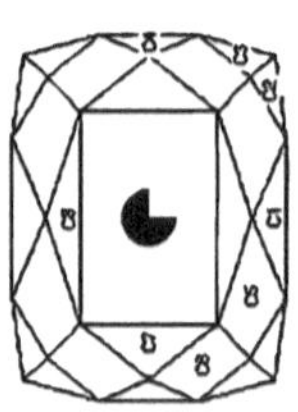 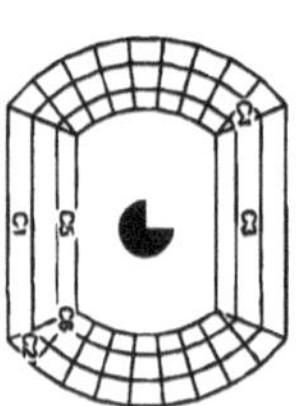

TURTLESHELLS FOR FALSIES:
A VISIT WITH MAVIS

She lives in the desert a few miles outside Barstow in an old Airstream trailer. In the dirt off the side of the Airstream there's a small table with two foldout wooden chairs shaded by a big umbrella. When I pull up, she rises from one of the chairs and steps out into the sun. Tall, the muscles in her arms and legs defined in the way of an athlete, lean, dressed in pastel blue shorts and a sleeveless yellow top, she's still a striking woman for being in her sixties. There's a dancer's fluid and suggestive grace in the way she moves that echoes her years as a Las Vegas showgirl in her twenties and thirties. Her skin wears a smooth and even desert tan. Her hair, a soft faded red in the late morning sunlight, is loose and moves in cadence with her walk.

In that much physical perfection it's not hard to notice something off about her breasts. They seem large for her. They ride uncommonly high. Their curvature is clumsy and unnatural. They lack the hang and counterswing you expect from breasts their size. They move instead like they're nailed to her chest. She motions me around the back of the Airstream where I park next to an old gray Jeep with a tarp thrown over the seats to keep the heat off. A propane tank and generator stand a few feet back. She's at the table waiting for me when I come around the side into the blast of the desert heat.

In the shade of the umbrella she takes her sunglasses off. Her gray eyes are kind but restless. Crow's feet fan back across her temples from the corners of her eyes and fine lines fan up into her lean cheeks when she smiles. It's a knowing smile. A smile that seems to know things about me that are probably true. The lines add the beauty of a life well lived to her native beauty. Her smile is quick but not without its share of wisdom and pleasant skepticism as she tells me about her life.

She was a cheerleader in high school. A showgirl seemed like a practical next step. But after fifteen years in Vegas, dancing in one casino hotel after another, she realized there was more to life than doing leg kicks in a chorus line. She wanted to let her life just happen. Let life come at her. Let it be spontaneous. Let its path be accidental, like the ball in a pinball machine, sent off in new directions with new possibilities one bumper or flipper to the next. Sometimes the bumpers hurt. Sometimes the flippers were mean. But there was always another bumper. Always another flipper. And usually there was a man involved.

She experienced the country. Worked all kinds of jobs. From her showgirl years she went into wrestling under the stage name Sadie Scissorlegs. From there, she says, she doesn't try to remember the order of things. But along the way she dealt blackjack in a Tahoe casino, moved furniture across seven western states, tended bar in Manhattan, worked for some power plants up and down the east coast. There were other places, other jobs, but she'd given me the flavor of her accidental life. When she'd seen and done enough, she moved here, to this old Airstream in the desert outside Barstow. She had a benefactor. A wealthy man who called her Gypsy and looked after her like his daughter. He'd made it possible for her to retire when she was ready to come off the road.

And so we come to this collection. In the shade of the umbrella Mavis tells me that she has always loved writing. Whether the occasional poem, brief prose piece, or short story, it has been the one consistent and indestructible attribute of who she is. The one attribute that has never been accidental but has always held steady. From the slimness of this collection you can tell that she'd written only intermittently. She was always on the move. But writing held everything together for her.

"You keep looking at my breasts," she says.

 It humiliates me.

"I'm so sorry."

"Look all you want. They're not real."

"I was wondering."

"Here. I'll show you."

"No. That's okay."

Ignoring my protest, she goes through an armhole of her sleeveless top, reaches inside, works something free, brings it out in the open.

"A turtle?"

"No, silly. Just the shell."

The plates of its back were intricately and boldly painted a multitude of bright and vivid colors that followed the patterns of the plates. Red. yellow, blue, turquoise, green, and more, colors whose names I don't know. White is reserved for those plates that indicate eyes, a nose, a mouth, the features of a face. Mavis rotates it to give me the full picture.

"I had them lined to keep from irritating my skin."

She turns it over to show me.

"It's beautiful," I tell her.

"Thank you. But I didn't paint them. I just bought them."

"Why? From where I sit, you don't need them."

"You mean falsies? No. I don't know why. I just drop them into my bra in the morning. I don't look for a reason."

She replaces and adjusts the shell almost as deftly as she removed it.

"Do you mind if I mention them in the introduction I'm writing?"

"No," she says, and shrugs when she looks at me. "Why should I?"

I'm here to help her collect and organize her work and showcase her writing in the book you're now holding.

"I've read every word of the 29 pieces you've given me. Their variety amazes me. They're nothing if not intensely human in one way or another. Some are playful while others are emotionally raw. Some tell stories while others are built on images that are not about anything except invoking a specific mood or emotion." I slowly shake my head. "I wanted your poem 'A Woman's Ass' to make sense before realizing it wasn't meant to. It just lets the images keep happening. But your versatility and range astonish me. This is all you have?" I say, indicating the manuscript I've laid on the table.

"For now," she says, a little shy for the praise. "Thank you for everything you just said. Are you thirsty?"

"I could use some water."

When she comes back I take a long swallow and continue. "What else really stood out for me," I say, "is the way you can switch between voices and points of view. First to second to third person. Male and female. You can write like a man as easily and believably as you can a woman. Like 'Covid House Arrest.' It's all a guy talking."

She thinks for a minute. "Yes. And I give him a house he's lived in for thirty years. I've never had a house unless I've rented it. Having one stops your life in its tracks. It's like looking ahead to dying.

But sometimes I have fun with writing like a guy. Switching back and forth. And sometimes a story will tell me how to write it." A soft smile, not without distance, comes into her face. "I've known so many men. I've loved them. They've loved me. I've put up with them and they've put up with me. I've laughed and cried with them and they've done the same for me. So it comes easy. And we've both known when it was time to move on."

To here. In the desert where there are no bumpers or flippers. Where the land is too flat, where it lacks the necessary incline, to let a ball roll in any direction. Where she can rest from an accidental life. A pinball life. A life well lived.

Max Zimmer, Editor

CONTENTS

OASIS

Katy tended bar and waited tables at a small place called the Toe
Hold on Beck Street on the northern outskirts of Salt Lake where the
tall thin candles of the refineries burned. It was a comfortable dive
of a place. A long homemade-looking bar scarred with circles and
cigarette burns, some mismatched tables and rickety chairs, a single
booth in back. In a tiny kitchen by the only restroom a Korean guy
named Hoon made burgers and chili and fries. A couple of dusty
bras left hanging from an overhead pipe let you know that the place
had seen better days. Wilder days. Now, in a neighborhood of refin-
eries, it had the feel of a neighborhood bar. When you first got there,
before you got used to it, there was always a scent of sulfur in the
cigarette smoke that hazed the lights. At one end of the back counter
stood a big jar of hardboiled eggs like the eyes of cows suspended in
pickle juice. A small wood picture frame hung on a nail on the wall
above the register. It held a grainy newspaper photo of two young
kids. A girl and a boy. The girl was older and had her arm around

the small shoulder of the boy. It looked like a studio portrait. Both of them were dressed in Sunday clothes. Both of them were smiling the bright wide open way that only kids can smile.

Some of the regulars worked at the refinery a short walk away. Some of the regulars wore suits that told you they were on their way home from office jobs in Salt Lake. The younger crowd mostly came in on Thursday, for karaoke night, and sipped on Cokes while they leafed through the DJ's binders and scribbled the songs they wanted to sing on paper slips. Most of them always sang the same song. There was the kid who howled his way through the Guns n' Roses cover of "Knockin' on Heaven's Door." The chubby girl who sang Janis Ian's "At Seventeen." Jeff the accountant who did "Desperado" in his western suit and string tie and cowboy boots. One of the refinery guys, a hulking older guy with a big gut and a bald head and a voice deep enough to feel in your bones, always sang "My Way." Everyone called him the Mayor. Nobody knew why. But nobody cared. It was a friendly and encouraging crowd where even the most tortured song was applauded. It was the one night of the week the place was full.

The DJ showed up at nine and stayed till closing time at one. He set up at the front of the room. He used one table for his machine and his small suitcase of karaoke disks, pushed back a couple of other tables to give himself and his singers room, set up his monitor, mounted two speakers on their tall stands, sang a couple of songs himself to prime the crowd. When the slips grew thin, when everyone was sung out, what was left of the crowd would always push Katy into singing the old Bread song called "It Don't Matter to Me." It was a song about letting someone go who needed time to be free, or needed to go out searching for themselves, or found someone who was better than her to take up with. It was a song about keeping an empty room and an open heart in case the searching brought them back together again. Time, she'd sing, was on her side. She'd wipe her hands on a bar towel, go up front, take the microphone, wait for the crowd to quiet down while the DJ cued up the song.

In her late twenties or early thirties somewhere, Katy was a big-boned woman who always wore overalls and one of her turtlenecks behind the bar, kept her thick dark hair clipped back behind her ears, and when she sang, sang with a crystal pure voice that made her seem small and fragile. She sang about letting someone go with a failed tenderness that held the heartache of a desolate angel. And if you listened when she sang the title line, how it didn't matter to her, you could tell she was lying. You could hear how much it mattered to her to have someone she loved go out searching for someone better than her. But she would let them go. She sang it knowing she didn't have the right to keep them if they wanted a shot at someone else. You could hear what it cost her to have surrendered that right.

When she finished the song, and let the microphone down to hang there in her hand for a minute before she smiled and gave it back to the DJ, the crowd would always wait. You could tell she'd moved them all the same way you'd been moved. The crowd waited while she walked back behind the bar to empty an ashtray or collected glasses from a table. And then they'd applaud and acknowledge her by quietly calling out her name.

She had a kid. A boy. His name was Mikey. Her shift was from three to closing. She'd pick him up from school and bring him in with her. She'd stick him in the booth or sit him at a table to do his homework. He wasn't shy. If something stumped him he didn't hesitate to ask one of the afternoon regulars for help. And they'd sit down with him. A couple of hours later Katy's mother would pick him up on her way home from work. You'd see the kid and wonder where the father was. You'd wonder, listening to her sing, if he'd found someone he thought was better than her. If he was the one she still kept an open heart and an open room waiting for. If time was really on her side. But that was before he started showing up.

"See you soon, Sweetie," Katy would always say, when her mother led the boy toward the door.

"My name's Mikey!" he'd shout, embarrassed and defiant.

"Okay, Sweetie. Your name's Mikey."

"Big Mike!" one of the afternoon regulars would say.

"Yeah!" the boy would shout. "Big Mike!"

And Katy would smile across the bar at him.

She had three trademark attributes. One was her eyes. They were this bright metallic blue you had trouble breaking away from when she looked at you. But her left eye had spears of green that gave her just the suggestion of something wild. Another attribute was the way she always wore a turtleneck. She had a collection of them—all plain but in all colors. You never saw her in anything else. The third attribute that stood her apart was her smile. It was there for anyone who came through the door, took a stool or a table, wanted a burger or a drink. It was there when someone hit on her. Guys who didn't know her thought she was smiling for some other reason. But they were quick to learn. Even when she was alone, washing glasses in the bar sink, coming up from the basement with a bucket of ice or a fresh soda tank, making a pot of coffee, it was there, at rest, always ready. And when you could take your eyes off the riveting look of her own, sneak a glance down at her smile, you could see the way her two front teeth were slightly crossed.

If you went there often enough, struck up provisional friendships with some of the night regulars, let them know you could be trusted, you'd start to hear guarded pieces of the story here and there, put them together. In high school she'd been a star. Cheerleader, yearbook editor, cellist in the school orchestra, class valedictorian, National Merit Scholar. She married her high school sweetheart, a basketball star, who'd gone on to become a highway patrolman. She went to the U and then law school and got a job with an established Salt Lake firm. For a couple of years she did well. Helped win some contingency cases. Brought in big money. Gave the firm a fresh young face and an innovative mind. Then everything went south. She defended a guy accused of shooting his wife in the face. The case was a slam dunk for a guilty verdict but Katy was convinced he was innocent. Returned missionary, temple marriage, two young kids. Somehow she got him off. A couple of weeks after walking out of jail he finished off the family. Took out his young son and daughter and then himself. Katy fell apart. She left the legal profession. The highway patrolman wanted no part of her. Drained of will, undeserving, she felt she had no right to anything, and let him have his way in the divorce. And he took it. The house and everything in it. Her lawyer's wardrobe and any other trace of her went the way of trash. She was left with the old Subaru she still drove. When she pulled herself together she left the state. When she came back she drove a cab, worked in a warehouse, had other jobs. And then one afternoon she showed up behind the bar at the Toe Hold.

Knowing her story made you a regular too.

A truck driver named Paul was one of the night regulars. He was a wiry little guy who delivered tanks of oxygen and acetylene and nitrous oxide and other gases to welding shops, hospitals, dentists, and other customers, and picked up the empties. Among his drops was a jazz drummer who kept a tank of nitrous in his bedroom. Just for laughs, Paul would say, and laugh this little laugh, like he'd just taken a hit of the gas himself. You could tell he had a thing for Katy. But he was married and Katy was out of reach. On karaoke night he'd always bring his wife Regina and sing "We've Only Just Begun" to her while she sat at a table blowing cigarette smoke through a quiet smile. You never knew what the smile was for. For how bad his singing was. For the way they'd already begun, long ago, way back in seventh grade. Or just because it made her feel famous and beautiful to be serenaded in public. On other nights Paul would be there on his own, like the other regulars, on a stool at the bar, tapping his cigarette into the glass ashtray Katy kept clean for him.

"I gotta have one of them pickled eggs before I go, Katy."

"Got you covered," she said.

"Regina's not gonna like that," said another regular named Al from the stool next to him.

"It ain't for Regina, Al. It's for the cops. In case one pulls me over and wants to check my breath."

'That's what they're for?"

"That's what I use 'em for. You wanna snap a cop's head back? Blow a little pickled egg breath in his face."

She hadn't known she was pregnant with Mikey when she left Utah. He wasn't the patrolman's kid. He was from some guy she'd met in the reckless twilight of the life she used to have. His name was Frank. He was a lean good-looking guy with a dirty grin and mean eyes and long hair and a honey-colored beard who rode an old Triumph motorcycle. Nobody knew what he did for work. Nobody asked. The consensus was that he rode around collecting dues from women he'd crossed paths with the way he'd crossed Katy's path. He started showing up a couple of months after Katy started working there. He'd come into the bar when Mikey wasn't there to see what she could give him. Katy would pour him a beer. He'd drink it looking back and forth at Katy and the tip glass she kept on a shelf among the dusty liquor bottles behind the register. She'd ignore him. The tip glass was for her and Mikey.

"Mikey was in here earlier," she'd say, smiling, running a rag across the bar in front of him.

He'd raise his head. Look confused. "Mikey."

"You know."

"Yeah," he'd finally say. "Sorry I missed him."

"Just letting you know."

"Buy me another beer?"

She'd rest her eyes on his face with a contemplative smile. And then she'd say, "You need to go, Frank."

He'd look at her, size her up, grin, get off his stool and go. You could hear him fire up his Triumph and ride off. And Katy would make sure everyone was topped off and then go out back for a smoke and sometimes a second one in the whine and howl of the refineries.

The regulars were quick to figure out that Frank wasn't the one she sang for. Tommy had known better from the start. He was a pipefitter who moved back and forth between the refineries repairing and replacing tanks, piping, valves, other equipment that needed cutting and welding. He kept his head shaved and sometimes wore his doo rag into the bar. Somewhere in his forties, muscular, Irish with an eager laugh in his round face, he always showed up with two or three old jokes you'd already heard.

"Hey. Katy. Got one for you."

"Yeah, Tommy."

"What do you get when you cross a black guy with a groundhog?"

"I've heard it, Tommy. It's not nice."

"Sorry."

"You need to stay off those fumes over there."

"You'd let me know if that guy ever caused you trouble, wouldn't you?"

"He's Mikey's father, Tommy."

"I know. I mean if he caused you trouble."

"He won't. I just need to leave that door open. For Mikey."

"Long as you're sure."

Her story about getting the killer off only to kill again had hit the papers and the tv news along with her real name. Everyone had read or seen it. She'd managed to dodge the cameras. All they had were high school yearbook photos. Leaving Salt Lake would end it. She called a law school friend who was practicing in a Nevada town called Jackpot. She packed up the Subaru and took Mikey and left.

Her friend helped her change her name and hooked her up with a mom and pop casino where she dealt blackjack and sometimes danced. She learned how to bartend. Her folks had moved too, to another suburb town across the valley where they could be anonymous again, and then her dad had died. A vein had let go in his head and flooded his brain. She moved back because her mother was alone and Mikey was her only grandkid. Her new name gave her cover. And the story about the killer she'd set free had run its course in the news.

When she used the register you'd sometimes see Katy raise her face to the framed photo of the smiling boy and girl on the wall. Sometimes just a glance. Other times she'd linger for a second before ducking her face to work the keys. Sometimes she'd close the drawer and just stand there, smiling back at them, before getting back to business. Being a regular meant that you knew who the kids were and what had come of them. But knowing who they were didn't mean you understood what they meant to Katy. There was the way they looked straight into the camera. Did she wonder if they'd looked that way into the barrel of the gun in their father's hand? Why had she hung their photo there? To remind herself of what? Of her place? To never go back to practicing law? Were they what she sang about? Were they the longing she gave the song? The lie she made of the line "it don't matter to me"? Did she expect them to come back? Was it them she kept her empty room and her open heart waiting for? Was she hoping they were just out searching for themselves? Hoping their searching would bring them back together with her? Hoping to rewind her life back to the time they were both alive enough to smile at her? In the end, what they mattered to her was guesswork, guesswork you kept to yourself, because the last thing you could do as a regular was talk about it. They were dead. Time was on her side. She could have all the time she wanted.

Harry was a retired doctor. He wasn't close to retirement age, but he'd made as much money as he'd ever need, and that was it. He'd walked away from his practice. He always showed up in a Hawaiian shirt and cargo shorts, even in winter, like he was on permanent vacation, like the Toe Hold was a clubhouse on a Florida golf course or a bar on a cruise ship. He got jokes from the regulars. Is there a doctor in the house jokes when someone had a hard time finding their way to the door. What got him the most jokes was his head of wild sand-colored hair. It was a tumbleweed of hair. The regulars joked about how flammable it looked. About how you couldn't light a cigarette within five feet of it or poof. About the fire extinguisher Katy had behind the bar.

Harry was interested in Katy too. But there was that song. Always in the way. It don't matter to me. That song whose longing, that song whose open heart and empty room, were waiting for someone or something back in her past. Everyone knew it. The song meant that you didn't hit on Katy. After getting burned a couple of times, after getting kidded about Katy setting his hair on fire, Harry knew it too. And that was when he became a regular.

"Another one, Doc?"

"One more. Thanks, Katy."

"This one's with me."

"Thank you."

Nobody knew where Katy and Mikey lived. They didn't live with Katy's mother because the neighbors would eventually get to know who she was and her mother would have to move again. She drove a ratty old forest green Subaru with rust eating through the lips of the wheelwells and along the quarter panels. She would come up Beck Street in the daylight of the afternoon, and at closing time, when the register was done, she'd disappear south down Beck again into the dark. One or two of the night regulars would stick around to see her out, wait with her while she locked up, and send her on her way with a slap on the roof of her car. The Mayor was always one of them. She always protested. Said she could take care of herself. Then roll her window down when she was buckled up in the driver's seat.

"Thanks, Mayor."

"You get home safe. That's all the thanks I need."

"You don't really need to do this, you know."

"What I need is to be able to sleep tonight."

The regulars kept that old Subaru running for her. Timing belt. Water pump. Wheel bearings. Brake pads. They'd figure out the problem a day or so ahead so they'd know what to get by way of parts. The next afternoon, they'd put it on jack stands in the parking lot, open the hood, get their tools out of their trucks, go to work. In winter they'd take it inside a maintenance shed at one of the refineries.

"Saw one of your taillights was out last night, Katy. I got you a new one."

"Thanks, Gary. I'll put it in later."

"Already in."

"I owe you one when that one's dry."

Harry liked to sing the Tom Waits tune "The Piano Has Been Drinking." He had fun with it, making it a performance, lurching and staggering around, exaggerating the alcohol slur, but he couldn't hit a note except by accident. He was all around the melody.

"So I hear you were a lawyer," he said one afternoon when he was Katy's only customer. In his hands was one of Hoon's big burgers. Hoon sat back in his usual place where the bar turned a corner into a wall. A cup of Hoon's chili stood off Harry's elbow. Katy held his eyes for a moment and then looked down. His forearms were hairy and sinewed where he'd laid them on the stained wood of the bar. With his burger in his hands he had the biggest knuckles she'd ever seen. She wondered briefly if he had arthritis. If he'd been a surgeon and his knuckles had made him give it up. But it was none of her business. Like what he'd just said was none of his. The whiskey glass on the coaster in front of him was empty.

"Still thirsty?" she asked him.

"I was just trying to see you in a suit," he said. "That's all."

"I was, Harry. Like you were a doctor once."

"No harm intended," he said. And then he said, "Yes. I'd like another."

"No harm taken, Harry."

One Thursday Frank showed up for karaoke. He sat at the back of the bar, next to where Hoon sat when nobody was hungry, looking through a binder. He walked up front and gave the DJ a paper slip. Then he went back and waited. The DJ never called his song. Even the DJ was on to him. Frank got the picture. He left that night before Katy sang. Al and Tommy, their backs to the bar, watched him go.

"What song you figure he wanted?" said Al.

"Money," said Tommy.

"Pink Floyd?"

"Yeah."

"How about Comfortably Dumb," said Al.

"That works too."

The best singer in the place, next to Katy and her one song, was a functioning drunk named Scotty. He was old school. He always showed up in the same white shirt, the same black tie and vest and slacks, his thin black hair slicked back and shiny with tonic. He moved furniture as a day helper two to three times a week depending on his immediate need for money. Thin, spindly, his hands shaky till a drink or two steadied them, he didn't look like he could carry more than an empty goldfish bowl, but the Mayor talked about seeing him hump a refrigerator up a narrow flight of basement stairs on his back.

Scotty came from a different time. A time of standards. Dance halls and big bands and show tunes. Night and Day. When Sunny

Gets Blue. I Loves You Porgy. Stormy Weather. Embraceable You. Someone to Watch over Me. Satin Doll. He brought in his own satchel of karaoke disks in case the DJ didn't have them. He could sing them all. And he sang them without looking at the monitor. Instead, he turned side to side, sometimes turned around, nodding to imagined musicians like he was fronting a real band. When he sang, the light fumbling stutter of his talking voice would disappear, and the water his eyes seemed to float in would clear away. The voice that came out of him was deep, confident, smooth as oiled silk. They called him the Mailman because of his satchel and because they couldn't believe the voice he brought to karaoke night was his. He was just delivering it.

Katy adored him. Sometimes she liked a song so much she'd take money out of her tip glass to buy him a drink and ring it up on the register. And you'd see Scotty leave her a tip big enough to more than cover it. He knew about Mikey too.

But as good as Scotty was, it was Katy who had to be goaded into singing, and her song was the closer every Thursday night. That she sang it with a smile let you know just how indestructible her smile was. But if time was on her side, the way the song said, her smile sometimes made it look like time was the only thing still on her side.

And then, late one Thursday night going into winter, time itself seemed to run out for her. The front door opened and a highway patrolman walked into the place. Tall enough to have to duck to get his round-topped hat through the door, gold beehive patches stitched to the shoulders of his dark brown tailored shirt, a holstered revolver on his belt. Most of the young crowd was gone. Only one table was occupied. It was Al and the Mayor. The bar was shoulder to shoulder with regulars. Even Paul's wife had moved from a table to a stool. Harry was in the middle of his Tom Waits drinking song. He saw the patrolman, stopped, got sober, stood there holding the microphone. The DJ killed the song.

"Hello, Levar," said Katy.

She finished opening a Bud and set it in front of Tommy. On a small plate pinned to the highway patrolman's shirt was the name that used to be her married name, the name she'd shared with him, till she'd changed it in Jackpot.

"Hello, Chris."

"It's Katy now," she said. Then she said, him being a cop, "All legal."

He looked at her.

"Katy," he said.

"I can show you my ID," she said, smiling.

The patrolman just looked at her.

"So you work here now," he said.

"How'd you find out?"

"I walked in and here you were."

"Here I am."

He kept his hat on his head. From under the felt disk of its flat round brim he looked her up and down. Like he could be looking for a reason to arrest her. Took in her face, her hair, her overalls, her turtleneck, the bar towel she was using to dry her hands.

"So how've you been, Levar?"

"Been good."

"Married again? Kids?"

"Nope. You?"

"I've got a son."

"Who's the dad?"

"Not you." She smiled. "That's all you need to know."

"Katy," he said. "I like it. Your name."

"Then it's a keeper."

"Last name?"

"Yep. It's gone. You're clear. I can't cause you any more grief."

He barely smiled. He ran his eyes down the row of people sitting at the bar and across the room. Only two people were looking back. A Mexican woman at the bar and a massive older man with no hair and a gut like a cow who'd just raised himself up from a table. The rest were watching Katy or looking at their drinks.

"Wish it was that easy," he answered, not looking at her.

To his right was a guy with a rawboned face and a cloud of sandy hair, wearing shorts and a Hawaiian shirt, a microphone hanging in his hand.

"You thirsty?" Katy said.

"Coke," the patrolman said.

She put down the bar towel, scooped ice into a tall glass, grabbed the Coke gun, filled the glass in squirts to keep the foam from flooding over, stuck a wedge of lime and a straw in it.

"Everything all right, Katy?"

It was the older man with the gut and no hair. He had a voice that felt and sounded as big and deep as his gut.

"Yes, Mayor," Katy said.

She set the glass on a cardboard coaster in front of the patrolman.

"These your friends now?" he said.

"They're my customers, Levar."

"They keep you out of trouble?"

"That they do."

"Keep you from getting other people killed?"

You could see the quick shudder of the shock go through her. Every face along the bar was watching them now.

"Don't, Levar."

"Kids, Chris. Shot in the face."

Katy lowered her head.

"Please, Levar. Just go."

A guy with thick shoulders and arms, a friendly face, a doo rag tied around his shaved head, got off his barstool and approached the patrolman.

"Excuse me," he said, quiet, pleasant, smiling. "You here to arrest someone?"

"Not yet," said the patrolman. "Why?"

"Make sure the liquor license is good?"

"Not my business."

"Any other official reason? Health inspection?"

"Why?"

"Well, if you're not, I think you just wore out your welcome."

"What?"

"She asked you to leave. That's her prerogative."

They looked at each other for a long while. Tommy never broke his steady smile. The patrolman finally glanced at his untouched glass, looked down the bar, looked at the older man still standing, looked at Katy.

"See you around."

And now the guy she'd called the Mayor came forward.

"Know why they call me Mayor?" he asked the patrolman.

"Tell me."

"Because I know everybody."

"Who's everybody?"

"Everybody who matters. So no, son. You won't be seeing her around. You won't come back and you won't go looking."

There was the morning long ago in Jackpot when she came home in the pre-dawn dark from the casino to find two guys in her apartment, ransacking the place, looking for money. They were obviously addicts. She gave them all the cash she had on her. It wasn't enough. One of them opened a straight razor and held it to her neck while the other one kept asking where the rest of her money was. Every time she told them she didn't have any there, the one with the razor would glide the blade across her neck, just enough to break the skin and leave a thread of blood. She didn't dare move. He had the steady surgical hand of a tattoo artist. They finally left. She closed the front door and made it to the mirror of her emptied medicine cabinet.

Her neck was webbed with strings of drying blood. She used a washcloth to dab and wipe the blood away. The cuts were too shallow to need stitches. But they would leave scars.

She remembered thinking maybe it wouldn't be so bad to die. Welcoming the idea of death. With her head held back hard against the sharp bones of a shoulder, the exposed skin of her neck pulled tight, she'd felt each cut of the razor like a kite string slipping through her hand. Death wouldn't be so bad. When it came, her body would release her like a kite, and her lifeless hand would let the string play out as she climbed and climbed and climbed, lighter than air, into the open sky. She was still pregnant then. Mikey was safe inside her. He would come with her. And they could be with the girl and boy she'd gotten killed. She could take care of them. She could protect them. The string that held each of them airborne to face the wind was infinitely long. They would have the whole sky. Free to dance, weave, dive, cavort, climb high again, free to go out searching with their colors vivid, bold, shimmering in the sunlight. It didn't matter to her. When their searching brought them back together with her, the way it always did when the song came to an end, they'd find her waiting. Time. It was always on her side.

After the highway patrolman left, Katy took his untouched glass, emptied it into the bar sink, set it with the other dirty glasses on the drain board. Then she turned to the register, took it in her hands, and looked up at the photo of the kids. The bar was quiet. She stood there looking, holding the register, like a statue. And then she dropped her head and stood there, not moving, her face down, and you couldn't tell if her eyes were open or she had them closed.

Paul's wife Regina finally got off her stool and went around behind the bar. She was plump and a head shorter than Katy. She stood next to Katy and put the flat of her hand on Katy's back. For a while she just left it there. Then she slowly started rubbing it in circles. Under her overalls and turtleneck you could see Katy's back and shoulders stiffen. And then start to shudder, over and over, as big silent sobs rolled in quakes up her back into her shoulders. Regina moved in close and took Katy in both her arms. The men at the bar watched in silence, scratched the backs of their hands, looked into their drinks. Katy finally let go of the register, stood up straight, turned to Regina, put her arms around her.

"Thank you. I'm okay."

Regina reached up and placed her open hand against the side of Katy's face.

"Yes," Regina said. "You are."

Katy picked up the bar towel.

"Katy?" the DJ called from his table at the front of the room. "Your song?"

"I'm sorry, Phil. Not tonight."

"Understood."

"Katy? W-w-would you mind if I s-sang it?"

She looked down the bar for Scotty. With his slicked back hair, in his black vest and tie, he was already off his stool, on his feet.

"I'd love that, Scotty," she said. "I would."

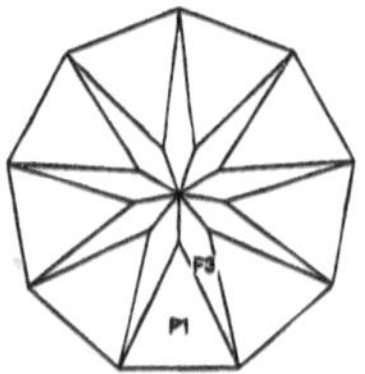

21

THAT YOU WILL AWAKEN

Spring is when the sun
takes off its raw glove
raises its warm hand
to my face to let me
feel rivers move again
in the hard veins of leaves
hear the wings of
the summer returning
and breathe the new dream
that you will awaken
having dreamed for me.

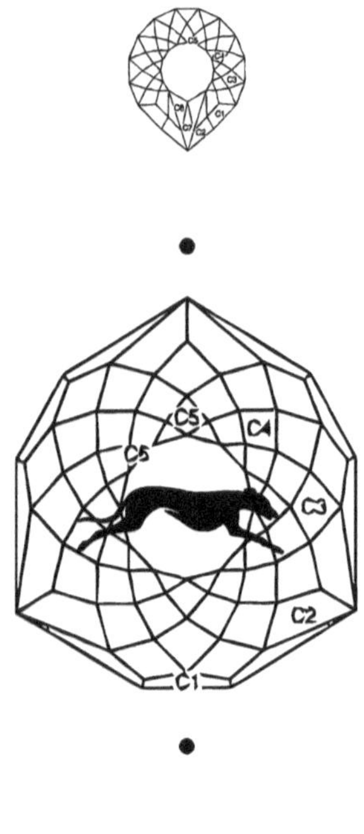

C5
C5
C4
C3
C2
C1

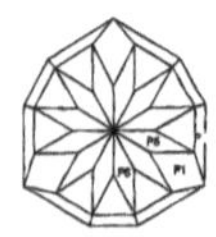

CITY OF UNCLES

In Seattle, early on Sunday on a stopover before leaving the States on another overseas assignment, he looks out the dirty window of the downtown room he took last night. Across the airshaft he sees himself reflected on the surface of a window identical to his. A diagonal crack in the glass runs like a fault line through the likeness of his face and the arm he's using to hold the shade aside. He looks away and suddenly wants to see a neighborhood. He goes through his duffle bag, finds his levis and sneakers, shakes the wrinkles out of a tropical shirt he's been carrying around, then packs his uniform and dress shoes in the bag and puts his shaving kit in on top of them. Leaving the bed unmade, he turns in his key at the desk, walks the couple of blocks to the Trailways depot, and stashes the bag in a locker. Outside the depot he catches the first city bus that comes along and rides it out to the end of its route. When the bus pulls off he finds himself on a sidewalk on a hillside street in one of Seattle's blue-collar neighborhoods. It's just past eight. In the wake of the empty bus the quiet surprises him. He starts walking. Two-story houses, maybe forty years old, small and sturdy and sided with asphalt shingles made to look like brick, line the quiet street. Hibachis sit on the dirt off the porches. Second-floor bedroom windows are open to the morning air but their sills are vacant. Tired old boats of cars are parked on some of the yards. A Buick Electra has its sun-bleached hood in the air, an Olds 88 has its big rear end on jack stands, and half the naugahyde has been scraped from the Landau roof of a Grand Marquis. Where the corner lots are vacant, he can tell from the paths worn through the weeds that kids play ball and ride their bikes in circles. There are no trees. Telephone poles carry their black wires through unobstructed air. From the sidewalk he can see the Space Needle rise above the morning haze of the downtown buildings. Somewhere down there is the cheap hotel where he slept and the depot where his stuff is lockered. What someone said on the plane last night was true. Seattle is full of uncles. He can smell them. In the mild air, he can smell the uncles who watch the kids, play with them, teach them how to let a bad pitch go. They've drawn him here, to this neighborhood, to this heart of Seattle's uncle country, to become an uncle himself. Half a block ahead he sees a redhaired woman in a black dress and green heels come hurrying out of a house, open a little chain link gate, and start walking briskly down the street. He sees a darkhaired guy in slacks and an undershirt come out behind her and hesitate at the gate. He hears the darkhaired guy yell something at the woman. The woman keeps going. He feels a breeze play through his tropical shirt while he watches the darkhaired guy throw his arms in the air, close the gate, go back inside the house. He hears the quivering slam of the storm door. He wonders if they both live there or if she's only spent the night. He listens to her quick heels on the sidewalk. Maybe she's angry. Or late for something. Or maybe the night she spent with the darkhaired guy has left her pregnant. He watches her red hair loosely ride the air as she goes on down the hill. And maybe this is it. Where his luck turns. With luck, he thinks, maybe nine months from now, she'll have a little girl with the same red hair. A year or two down the road, when he passes through the States again, maybe her little girl will ride on his knee and like the toys and clothes he brings her from the places he's been stationed. Maybe a few years later she'll want to know about boys. He'll sit there with his tie loose, his duty cap tossed nonchalantly on the kitchen table, her little shoulders cradled in his arm. He'll think back briefly to the darkhaired guy in the undershirt, and he'll tell her then that boys have scrambled eggs for brains, and waffles for hearts, and Aunt Jemima's pancake syrup for blood. He'll wink at her redhaired mother, still not married, heavier but still beautiful, when she smiles at him from her chair across the table. Outside, on a day like this, every other uncle up and down the street will be coming home from church to pull on a fresh-washed teeshirt, crack a can of Olympia or Pabst, open the hood of the car, use lighter fluid to get the hibachi off the front porch going, roar for all he's worth as a kid steps up to the plate to face the uncle hefting the softball in his thick bare hand. He can smell the teeshirt. He can taste the beer. Through the open window of the kitchen, he can hear the soft curse from the yard next door, and the dull chiming of the dropped wrench falling through the engine compartment to the grass.

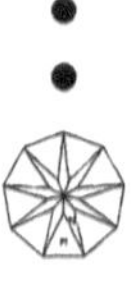

AFTER YOU SET YOUR HEAD ON FIRE

The way your father waits for the bus to the slaughter
house outside the house each morning with his brown shoes tied

The way your father drowns in the noisy snoring of his
daughter's dreams at night through the thin rock of unpainted wall

The way your father runs across the weeds of the fields
in October afraid he will never quite get far enough away from you

The way your father lets the engine of the mower idle
while he dumps the catcher of all the presents you have given him

The way your father can taste bark in his blood when
he strips the tree in the yard for food in winter with his fingernails

The way your father says he can stare at the sun until
his eyes burn black and still catch a sparrow in flight with his teeth

The way your father can eat an apple ignorant of how
it terrifies you that he will be dead when you are forty or fifty or sixty

The way your father can sit in a chair and smell like a
river of people you will never know but know have held you naked

The way your father touches your thigh with the side
of his hand when he shifts into third and your mother tells nobody

The way your father will always pull off the highway if
one of two things happens:

> The first is every time a turkey vulture asks him for directions
> to his grandson's funeral

> The other is every time you tell him that you're carsick again

> The first thing never happens

The way your mother knows exactly what you should
get when you add two and two and the answer is a banker's hand

The way your mother hollows out the two fresh halves
of a zucchini and fills them with the heads of her daughter's dolls

The way your mother spends the afternoon in her bra
in the chaise beside the stream with your father's beard in a bottle

The way your mother can walk the edge of the roof in
a wind as fast as the warm venom of a rattler racing for your heart

The way your mother uncovers the silver hook of her
bridge when her lips pull back off her teeth in an animal's laughter

The way your mother eats wild berries with the best of
them in the dream you love about the house where all women live

The way your mother can reach inside your stomach
to grab how you've had to swallow the lie about leaving her again

The way your mother cries out when a glass breaks in
her grownup hand in the warm buoyant water of the porcelain sink

The way your mother bicycles off down the hill to the
store while they talk of snow coming on the radio before tomorrow

The way your mother will always pull off her stockings
if one of two things happens:

> The first is every time the shadow of a candle passes like the
> last man through her room

> The other is every time you tell her that she's beautiful again

> The other thing never happens

The way you wear your father's broad shoes and they
fit you like the cages of turtleshells when you go running after him

The way you finish the dishes after the blood of your
mother's hand has colored the suds the muddy pink of the sunset

The way you wrap your blazing hand around the neck
of this toothless thing you come to learn was your first ejaculation

The way you wade through the flood of the basement
to rescue your wife's last kiss from the trunk where her wedding is

The way you drive through the headlights of a deer at
fifty five the night your father accuses you of having molested him

The way you move furniture in the rain in April for rent
for the month of May for the place where you eat from your knees

The way you were told that this is what happens to a
widow's dog if it isn't advertised in the classified ads on Saturday

The way you set your head on fire and the last of the
kids to ever have said they hated you starts to whimper in his yard

The way you know you've been to this city before but
with a different haircut or shirt or place of birth or something else

The way you will always look the way you look tonight
if one of two things happens:

      The first is every time you play this song where your children
      are baskets of ripened fruit

      The other is every time you play this song again from memory

One or the other thing is always happening

THE PENNY STACKER

Back in school I'd sometimes hang out with a guy who could balance a penny on its edge on top of another penny on its edge and another penny on top of that penny and on and on. I don't know how he did it. I looked for wires, I looked for glue, I looked for any other gimmick he could be using. I searched the Internet for a standing a penny on top of a penny trick. I came up empty. In the end I figured it had something to do with gravity. Or magnetism. There was the way he would move his open hands in different wave patterns up and down either side of his growing column. Could his hands and fingers give off that kind of controlling power? Could they suspend or manipulate gravity? Could they exert tiny magnetic fields? The copper and zinc that make up a penny aren't magnetic. I know because I tested one. Did his pennies have a steel core? I asked him once if I could contribute a penny of my own. Without a word he took and made it the next penny in his stack. It held. So much for magnetism. Gravity was a lot scarier. Gravity—the suspension of gravity—was Einstein country. And I had no idea how to test for it. So it remained an open possibility.

Whatever it was—it was a fragile power. He couldn't do it outside because the lightest breeze would keep him from getting even the first three pennies to work. And if someone bumped the cafeteria table he was using, the whole delicate construction would fall apart, and come raining down in a shower of pennies. He couldn't do it with other coins. He'd tried them all—nickels, dimes, quarters, half dollars, dollars. It was only possible with pennies. "It's not a trick," he told me, when I asked him once. "I've tried to figure out how it works since I was old enough to figure things out. I was just born this way." That didn't make sense. "Born this way" meant a lopsided head or skinny legs or blond hair or short a couple of toes.

He tried to make money once off his special skill. Bet, say, a buck or two that he could do it. The more he promised to stack the higher the bet would go. But his skill had a mind of its own. It didn't like going commercial. He couldn't get off the ground floor. Not even the first penny. Not only did he have to ante up a buck or two—he'd get laughed at or beat up in the process.

I bring him up because he recently got hold of me through my stage name and my old website. "It wasn't easy finding you," he said.

"That was the idea," I said. I could feel the lure of the penny trick start tugging at me again.

"I watched a couple of your videos," he said. "Pretty sexy stuff. Lots of skin."

"That was in another life," I said.

He thinks it over. "You could have stayed in touch," he said. "I thought we were buddies."

"We were," I said. "We just didn't run with the same crowd."

"I grew a beard," he said. "I look like Lincoln now. It goes with the pennies."

It took me a minute to get the connection. I tried to imagine the guy on the phone with Lincoln's beard but it wouldn't come.

"You mean Abraham. The guy on the penny."

I didn't hear anything. I wondered if he was posing for me, looking into a mirror, at the other end of the line.

"Did you hang out with me just for what I could do with pennies?" he said.

That hit the nerve he wanted. I just about fell apart from the urge to see him do it one more time.

"I don't know," I said. "I don't remember."

"You don't remember," he said, after a long pause. "You know what?" he said, after another long pause.

"What?" I finally said.

"I feel used," he said. "Really used." Then he said, "I figured out how it worked. With the pennies. I got hold of you to tell you what you were always snooping around to know. Too bad you never will." And hung up.

I knew he'd mentioned his name when I answered the phone. Now I'd forgotten his name a second time and lost him again. His Caller ID said Unavailable. No number. But he was right. I'd hung around him for what he could do with pennies. But isn't it that way it is with any friendship? You can like one thing—just one thing—about someone enough to make friends with them? I kept the phone to my ear, hoping he'd regret the way he'd talked to me, just pick up his phone again and find me there, waiting.

It's been rumored that the day will come when the government stops making pennies. They would still stay in circulation. Millions of them would be floating around out there for a long while. But the day of the penny would be over. They would peter out, end up in the charity jars at convenience store counters, and be forgotten. Tricks that involved pennies would gradually fall out of favor and become obsolete themselves. I wondered what my friend would do. If he'd shave. After a while I just stopped caring.

PREDATOR

for Richard Whitney

Running out on what you could have once called home,
a woman cries out from the bag of her face at her bedside.

Sad as a whisper of love from this thing you have killed,
her voice is the heartbeat of everything you should avoid.

You were beautiful, you tell her, while it lasted. And she
learns how to scream in secret but not yet quite so well

that she can hide her open mouth behind her eyes. The
motion of your leg keeps coming back from the time you

remember having it. Cripple, the mouth of pain in your
side like a writhing shell to which you put your ear, you

listen to your future call you off, then back again, then
off. The rusted Plymouth you will follow to its grave is

idling on the edge of everything you understand. Leave.
She was beautiful, remember, but only while it lasted.

It has to end where you still know what it means to eat
a brittle taco while you watch the parking lot. There on

the nubbled bedspread is the naked skin of your failure
to hope for things just as they are. There on the nubbled

bedspread is the last girl you think you had a temporary
hand in making beautiful. You hope, instead, not for an

end to your doing this, but always for what stands there,
beyond the bleak victory of leaving, to stand there again:

Where your leg comes back to you, briefly, as a mother
you have punished someone for, where you can watch a

movie at two a.m. that night in the next motel through
the temporary rifle sight of a pair of shoes. And you—

you with the wind of your life behind you pointing you
always forward from love—are beautiful while it lasts.

OSWEGO WINTER

I once followed a guy named Kenny to an upstate New York town called Oswego. He was a welder and pipefitter—a so-called "boomer"—who traveled from one nuclear power plant to another during planned outages to do welding repairs on the piping systems. It was a risky job because much of the piping was hot. As in radioactive. The guys had to wear dosimeters that measured the accumulated radiation they were picking up. When the meters reached a certain limit the guys had to be pulled off the job for their own good. They had other guys whose job it was to initially go into a work site to see how hot it was. They were nicknamed glowboys. Kenny, the guy I followed, was contracted for a year. There was a college there so I decided to take a couple of classes. And I got to know the town.

Oswego had around 25 feet of snow over the course of the first and only winter I was there. For those of you who count snow in inches, that comes to around 300 of them, but I'll have more on that later.

The college was a State University of New York campus right along the shoreline of Lake Ontario. Much of that ridiculous snowfall was what they called lake effect, where a storm blows across the lake from Canada, picking up more and more moisture. Whiteouts were common on campus. Ropes were strung from building to building so students wouldn't get lost in the blinding swirl of heavy snow.

The wind could be fierce. On particularly windy days the school had a "small person warning." I forget what the weight limit was, but if you weighed, say, under a hundred pounds, you were officially told to stay home from class and the absence wouldn't be held against you. Ice would form along the shoreline where the lake wasn't deep. One of the warnings the teachers gave in my classes was not to wander out onto the ice. It was deceptive. On the surface it could be smooth. But the underside was scalloped out by the driven underlying waves to where the ice could be several feet thick but could suddenly change to only the thickness of an inch or less. Still, there were students who persisted, despite the warnings. They considered themselves invincible. Or they were drunk or stoned or both. A student would simply stop showing up for class. In fact he wouldn't show up at all till spring, miles away around the east end of the lake, where he'd wash ashore, his eyes and ears and nose and fingers nibbled away by fish.

Oswego had a dramatic history. It had started out as a shipping town. You could see its former wealth in the old mansions of affluent neighborhoods. You could see it in commanding stone churches like Saint Mary's with its high bell tower and steeple. Then New York built the Erie Canal connecting Lake Ontario to Lake Erie and the rest of the Great Lakes. And Oswego lost its status as a shipping center. You'll hear old timers say, with sadness and resentment in their voices, that if it weren't for the Erie Canal, Oswego would have been Chicago. The once wealthy and vibrant town that could have been

Chicago declined and started to decay. Other economic opportunities had to be found. Two big ones eventually came along.

First, the town had long been host to a small teacher's college. Then in the sixties came Governor Rockefeller's push to build campuses across the state as part of the State University of New York system. The old teacher's college suddenly found itself at the center of a sprawling four-year college complete with dormitories and a broad offering of majors. It turned out to be an economic boom for the town. Students swelled the population by a third or more when school was in session. Abandoned mansions were subdivided into apartments or picked up by sororities and fraternities. The second economic opportunity? Around the same time, two nuclear power plants—Nine Mile Point and Fitzpatrick—were constructed five miles east of town on the shoreline of Lake Ontario where they could draw cooling water from the lake.

I should give you a demographic map of the town. The Oswego River, one of those rare American rivers that flows north, divides the town into a west side and an east side before it spills into Lake Ontario. The campus, along with neighborhoods of student rentals, is on the west side. The nuclear plants, along with the workforce who maintain and operate them, are on the east side of the river. I was there during the anti-nuke movement. Between the college on one side and the nukes on the other, the town felt like the camps of two warring armies. I went to a party once in the middle of that winter at a student apartment that took in the entire second floor of one of the mansions. It was supposed to be an anti-nuke party. A couple of stereos were blasting rock music at a volume that shredded the sound from the speakers. In subzero weather every window in the place was wide open. The furnace had to be close to meltdown in its effort to keep up. Every light in the place looked like it was on. I stayed maybe five minutes. I left puzzled. If you want to put nukes out of business, I thought, start conserving power. Shut the windows. Turn off some lights. Turn down the stereos to where people can hear each other. Later that same winter I fell in behind an old pickup truck on the east side of town with a tailgate bumper sticker that read "May all you anti-nuke bastards freeze to death in the dark." I wanted to buy that guy a beer. I told Kenny about it and he went out and got the same sticker for his truck.

What did the town do to handle 25 feet of snow that wouldn't start to melt till the end of March? There was heavy salting—the reason cars started showing rust around the wheelwells before they were three years old. There was the town rule against overnight on-street parking from November to April. At night, the streets theirs, the heavy equipment came out to play. Huge snow throwers arced the snow high onto banks that grew higher with each successive storm. Payloaders loaded snow into dump trucks. The trucks hauled it down to the lake to dump it and return for more. The rule was strict. I saw where the side augers of a big thrower once laid bare and shaved off the entire side of an illegally parked car.

But even the heavy equipment—the red and yellow dinosaurs of the night—couldn't keep up. Sidewalks disappeared under growing banks of snow. Everyone walked in the street where the slow buildup of snow, heavily salted, was like walking on cake dough when it needs more water. Cars had rods twenty to thirty feet tall installed on their front bumpers, tipped with red flags, so you could see them coming over the high walls of the intersections. I couldn't remember the last time I'd put snow chains on a car. Now a pair went on the back tires of my rusty but trusty old BMW.

Many of the students came from upstate towns and cities. But a good share of them also came from Long Island. It didn't make sense to me. There had to be a hundred colleges closer to their home towns than Oswego was. Then someone clued me in. A few years earlier, Playboy had named Oswego State as one of the top ten party schools in the country. Party school. A light came on in my head. That was the draw. Oswego had 192 bars for a resident population of less than ten thousand that was augmented, during the school year, by a student population of maybe three thousand more. The bars came in all shapes and sizes. From bars with live music to attract students to ramshackle neighborhood bars where the locals drank.

To this. One night, walking along a neighborhood street, I saw a neon Molson sign in the dark picture window of a house. This was new. Someone's house. I figured what the heck. The door was unlocked. I walked into a darkened living room that had been converted to a simple bar. A woman greeted me from behind it. "Welcome," she said. "Come on in." "It's okay?" I said. "If you're old enough," she said. I took a stool. Every other stool was empty. I asked her for a Molson. She put one in front of me. "Need a glass?" she asked. "No thanks," I said. She set an ash tray where I have could have reached it if I smoked. Maybe half the bottle later I heard a baby's cry coming from upstairs. "Excuse me," the bartender said, "I'll be right back." I sat there listening to her quiet the baby. There was an ancient cash register on the back wall. There was stemware hanging from a ceiling rack. There was a mirror on the wall behind the cash register where I could look at my face. I didn't belong here. I knew that. But this was her house. I couldn't just leave. I watched myself finish my beer. I waited for her to come back down so I could thank her and say goodnight.

And to this. At a local place one night, I struck up a conversation with an old timer, and got to where I could ask him why people around here drank so much. "Notice how wet it always is?" he said, meaning the rain and snow. "If we didn't stay as wet on the inside, we'd warp." I laughed, and looked around, and saw a younger guy leaned back against a pole, his fly open, his shirttail in his hand, a blissful look on his face while a dark patch spread like octopus ink from his crotch down his right leg.

A top ten party school in a party town. Hold on there, Playboy. The truth was that unlike a real party school—say in a Florida beach town—there was nothing to do in Oswego in the wintertime but drink. Anyone with an apartment, a stereo, and a keg in the bathtub could throw a party. Kids would come. They'd stand around, often in their parkas, a plastic cup in their hand. One night, waiting in someone's hallway for my shot at the bathroom, I asked the kid in front of me if he was having fun yet. "Yeah," he said, with a rueful Long Island smile. "Almost like being alive."

DEATH OF A REFRIGERATOR

It's cold in here
it whistled one morning.
So because we're friends
and live in the same house
and look out for one another
I called for the repairman.

No one came that night.

In the morning I heard it wail
So did you send for him?
Its voice was faint.
Its cubes were pale and watery.
Its light was weak.
Its temperature was rising.
And the way it rattled scared me.
I've heard how things rattle
just before they end for good.

I deserved better. I couldn't say it
but to get even
I took out all my food
left its shelves and bins empty
gave it some baking soda

put my chair in a corner
and ignored it the rest of the day.

That night again no one came.

In the morning
it was all white
with black crud lining its lips
During the night
it had spit up its motor.
When the repairman came
with a dust mask
and a hand truck
like a stretcher with wheels
I heard him say compressor.

I glanced up when he left.

I should find a new one
one with those space-age shelves
and lighted pull-out baskets
and bins with windows where
the tomatoes are always red
where the baloney is always
this rosy pink
and water and ice are there
without opening the door
or one that's second hand
but in good condition.

But there's a time for everything.

And in the meantime

there is no wax on the floor
where the old one stood
only black strings of lint
strands of fur under a stiff dog
black dents in the linoleum
left by wheels
that never took it anywhere
never showed it the living room
or a sunrise from the porch

It wasn't what you would call a life.

BILLY

Somewhere between one and two in the morning, on the round dirt crest of Little Mountain, Billy hears the shrieking hammer of a wide open engine from the dark canyon down below him. Someone's tearing up Emigration. Coming up Emigration hell bent for leather. The sudden leap in pitch of a downshift. The wail of rubber trying to hold a curve. The lower growl of an upshift as the engine reaches deep for torque. The sound made huge and furious as it echoes off the hills along the open throat of the canyon. Billy opens the driver's door to his Plymouth, gets out, stands there in the rocky dirt and listens. He hears the girl murmur from the front bench where he left her, her shirt unbuttoned, her breasts these luminous ghosts, amber in the moonlight. Now, when he glances around, sees them illuminated by the dome light in the roof from his open door, she's pulling her bra back up, her teeshirt back down over them.

"What're you doing?" she says. "Taking a pee?"

"No." His own shirt unbuttoned, untucked, loose on his shoulders. "Just seeing what this is."

In the warm moonlight of the summer night, the dirt hills that rise sloping toward him are silver except where patches of scrub oak lie in stains of spilled black paint across them. He can start to see it now. Just the pale elusive glow of its headlights as they rake the far side of the canyon. And the sound. If sound was fire, he thinks, the whole canyon would be blazing. Here and there, where the hills are shallow enough to let him see deeper into the canyon, the white blades of its headlights slash back and forth as they trace the twisting road along the black vein of the canyon floor. The distance makes the sound lag behind what the car is doing. By the time he hears the tires its headlights are already well out of the curve. He can hear rage in the engine, rage in the downshifts and upshifts, rage in the tires, raw and mean and crazy, because only something this raw and mean and flat out crazy could come up Emigration Canyon this fast and hard and wild.

The girl slides across the bench and out the driver's door behind him, stumbles on the rocky dirt, stands next to him straightening her twisted peasant skirt. Like she's expecting company. Like she's expecting whatever's coming to stop for a friendly visit and take in the view. He won't. Billy knows that.

"The cops?" the girl says, running her fingers through her hair to take the tousles out of it.

Billy doesn't look at her. The cops, he's thinking. And wonders what her name is. If she told him when he picked her up on State and she parked her smoking Falcon in the South High parking lot to ride up here with him.

"Too crazy for the cops," he raises his voice to tell her, the engine closer now, louder, in his chest. Then he says, "It ain't a V8 either."

Wondering what it is. This demon crazy fast. This pedal to the metal. Who's behind the wheel. He sees its headlights reach the end of the canyon where the hills start giving way to the steep side of the mountain. When it starts the climb he loses sight of it but can hear it coming up the switchbacks, the letup of the engine for the downshift, the wail of the tires as it takes a hairpin, the upshift and the lower howl of the engine as it reaches deep for torque again on the uphill straight to the next hairpin. He looks back into the dark where he brought the girl up the road a while ago. Hopes where he's looking is where he'll see it make the summit. It isn't long. And then it's there. The headlights split the horizon from the sky. The engine breaks free of the echo of the canyon. Suddenly fierce, naked, its shriek cracks the night wide open. The girl cries out and covers her ears. Billy relishes the noise. Opens his mouth to it. Lets it flood his chest. Goes to put his thumb in the air but watches the car streak past like he isn't there. Its top is off but he can't make out a driver. Its body is dark and dull and low and too fast through the moonlight to give itself away. He follows its taillights. The quick red blink of its brakelights and the fire out its tailpipe as it slows and downshifts for the curve that takes it off the summit. Just a straight pipe, Billy's thinking, feeling as much as hearing it, the hoarse wide open drag strip crackle as it upshifts and looks for torque again. Whoever's behind the wheel of whatever kind of car it is has rage whose hunger he can only guess at.

"Jesus," he says. "He's hauling ass."

"You weren't doing so bad yourself," the girl says.

Billy almost smiles. Still watching it blaze down the long dark winding ribbon of the road that will take it down off the mountains and hills onto Interstate 80 where its four broad lanes descend down Parley's Canyon. Where the only traffic this late at night are semis coming down into the city. Or just passing through.

"Your ears okay?" he says.

"What was it?"

"Couldn't make it out."

"Break over?" she says, taking his arm, pushing the soft give of her breast up against it. "Can we get back to . . . business now?"

If he even told her his own name back in the lot where they left her Falcon. He follows it into the distance now. Just the sound and the random flash of fire out its tailpipe and the rake of its headlights as it rides the dark descending snake of the road along the silver hillsides. But he can feel its pull. He doesn't want to let it go. He wants to know what it takes to feel rage that clean and crazy. Even when it reaches the floor of Parley's and the access road to the Interstate. Even when he loses it to the hammering of the semis coming down Parley's using the brakes of their engines to keep their loads from running out from under them.

THURSDAY

The station burns to the ground and the rafters fall. Dorothy wakes from her nap and talks to the radiator while she starts making coffee. The stairwell has burned away from around the stairs. Three steel flights of stairs are clear of everything—walls and windows and ceiling—and stand up from the rubble of the station like a cantilevered chimney, a precarious rock formation, a sculpture commemorating the United Stairmakers of America. Three flights of stairs to nowhere. On the top landing, a man looks periodically at his watch, restlessly paces the ashen square of concrete, watches the bright sky. He may be waiting to board a helicopter or plane that hasn't yet arrived or has already departed. Below him, in ashes, lie the three floors of the station through which the stairs once led. One office is still intact. He sees a woman with no hair, dressed in a sooty turquoise sweater and skirt, leaning over the water cooler, filling the coffee pot. "Excuse me," he calls down to her. "Is this Thursday?" He waits, looks fitfully at the sky, calls down to her again. "Hey! Lady!

Is this Thursday, or are you bald?" Dorothy looks around for the voice, sees nobody, and goes back to filling the coffee pot with water. She tries to ignore the smell of smoke and ash around her, the mild breeze disturbing the paperwork on her desk, her keyboard basking in sunlight. Its ceiling gone, the office reminds her of the time she rode to the falls in the back of an Impala convertible, let her hair down, gave herself to the son of the farmer her brother dug potatoes for. Ricky? Randy? Has it been that long? What was his last name? She murmurs her questions softly in the direction of the radiator. "Hey!" the man yells down from the landing. "Hey, lady! Thursdays are for everybody! Not just you!"

COVID HOUSE ARREST

It's one in the afternoon on a Monday that happens to be Memorial Day. The grill stands covered and idle on the deck. The cushions for the outdoor furniture remain stacked in the basement where they've been since last November. The dog sleeps on its belly to absorb the cool of the planks. Traffic on Facebook is dominated by tributes to soldiers who didn't make it home and by posts about the pandemic. The young leaves hang still in the trees in the dead calm of the air. Nobody visits. Nobody calls. Nobody's going anywhere. I wonder whether it's too early for a glass of summer wine. There's plenty to do around the house and in the yard. I'm just not in the mood. It's a holiday.

A garage sale comes to mind. I wonder if I should have one. Empty out the house and put everything out front. Leave signs leading from the main road. Make everything free. From knickknacks to mattresses. Keepsakes. Chests and nightstands and dressers. From televisions to sofas. From pots and pans and dishes to lamps and the pictures on the walls. Tools. Metric and American. The lawn mower and snow thrower to a set of golf clubs and collapsible car show chairs. From hutches to tables to desks. Clothes. Shoes. Dresses. Suits. China. Crystal. Piano and trumpet. Exercise equipment. Computers and printers. Filing cabinets and everything inside them. The fridge too. Everything but what we're wearing. From medicine to firewood. Leave the house as I found it—empty like before. Everything free except for a couple of toilet paper rolls.

Leave the house as empty as I found it. What a concept. I wonder if I'm sitting on the answer to time travel. If emptying the house would take me back close to thirty Memorial Days ago to the day we took occupancy. How much shorter the tall oaks around the house would be. If the neighbors would change back to who they were back then. If the cars would too. If I'd have to take on a mortgage again. Build another replica Porsche Speedster. Write these books again. And if the trip through time, as Einstein theorized, would leave everything warped.

My girl comes out to the deck.

"What's up?" she says.

"I'm on a plane," I tell her.

"What?"

"Yeah. This is really cool."

"What's cool?"

"I'm the only passenger."

"Where are you going?"

"You tell me, Mavis. You're the flight attendant."

"Oh?"

"Yeah. Bring me another Chardonnay."

"Put on your mask first."

This is how you lose it. Slow. No pain. Comfortably numb.

A WOMAN'S ASS IS A SOMETIME WONDROUS MOMENT

Stake truck burning a tire
trying to hold
back the hard air of an accident
against the hill of a train
An old bus bearing hard left through
the hole worn into the rock of your
president's canyon hideaway
in northern Arizona coming
off the sandstone monoliths
where the Rockies die with the
sun on the prone red prairie
desert valley of the Reservation

Ansel roaming through the shoebox after
the smell of the fire lays him nose down
on the wild carpet of his wife's vagina
in the burned house of his town
A woman's ass is a sometime wondrous
moment to hold against one's ear
for the interval a drumskin quivers
with the brush of a pig's damp tail
Oh Jesus
Let me live in vain

Bob will dance on daffodils tomorrow
And his wife will sing a hymn
While Sam the barber starts a car on
the river by lighting a match to his ear
and crying "run, run, run"
And Joncie the goddess of steering
will eat her hair off a stick Oh Jesus
Let me live in vain
Oh Jesus let it rain
Oh Jesus have it run again
Oh Jesus keep us sane

A woman's ass is a sometime wondrous
moment
Wondrous is the moment when, held
in your palms, it forms the cup of an
offer of prudent love to the sunrise
(how the wind is easy on the dew)
Hard compressed air of an accident
when the brakes are smoke in the wet
dawn of a child's roaring ear

In the rear of the dark bus the open
door to the bathroom swings wantonly
against the heavy leg of the Navajo
sprawled and asleep on the toilet
Homeward bound where some
woman he knows will pick the
shards of a broken vodka bottle
from his tongue and throat and teeth
Homeward bound
at the end of a string off the cuff
of his new Pendleton jacket

the tag that will tell some woman
he knows how to clean it skates
and dances like Bob
across the back of his heavy hand
with the dead rapture of a marionette

Will he raise turtles when he retires
from the long career of this bus ride?
Will the woman boil kerosene like
the tag says?
Oh Jesus
when we let it rain
Oh Jesus when we let you make it rain

Off the highway out across the
red sagebrush floor of the
Arizona reservation
two sheep lead a Navajo woman
in the direction in which
she herds them
Like the burning mast of a raft her
skirt trails out in the fiery orange
wind of the sunset behind her
Will she grind corn tonight in the bowl
of her father's skull?
Does she wear the necklace of his toes?
On the bus
from the dark bench in the back where
a man's fist quietly wrings itself and
the paper bag that held the bottle does
not hold the vomit
someone turns the chamber of a woman's
heart until it is emptied of shells

and then hands it back to her

"You could tie my wife to a stake
and shave her" says the barber "with
less gasoline than a lizard holds"
Oh Jesus knock again
Oh Jesus stay with me in vain
Oh Jesus truck and bus and train
and a child's brutal singing
Sings Ansel's wife to the turquoise
bird in her husband's toothless
hand

Dance, Bob, because you are
who you are
because you are Jesus for the same moment
every afternoon
and because
a woman's ass a moment wondrous also
is a sometime hairless thing.

JIMMY

He was this rambling ragtag happy-go-lucky street guy who was always around the neighborhood of 30th Street. He wore busted-out workboots, unlaced, and he walked with this huge goofy swinging stride that made me think of Johnny Appleseed. And he moved. Full of purpose, like he had somewhere to go, he'd weave through people with the easy grace of a sailplane, his big tan canvas overcoat riding the wind he left behind him. His hair was this standout mop of dusty electrocuted-looking dreadlocks. He was the happiest guy I knew. In a city where you didn't openly grin, he was always grinning, this big meaty grin that animated his entire face, and his laugh was always there, ready to go, like an engine idling back behind his grin. Just call me Jimmy, he said, when I asked. He never asked back. One day, light rain falling, I ran into him on 31st. He was using a small bright yellow umbrella with a couple of busted spokes and a chrome stub of a handle. In the weird light underneath it, his brown skin took on highlights of iridescent green, and I realized that he'd started to call me Ricky.

He was from Virginia. I figured a small town because that was the feel he gave a neighborhood that didn't have much feel—like a block or two away, in any direction, there could be an orchard, a field, a shady place to drop a fishing line. Our conversations were brief, on the surface, so I never knew much else. How he made his way to New York. Where he lived. If or where he worked. I never saw him panhandle. I knew he didn't deal. I could tell he had a place to shave. But he wore that overcoat year round—even in the thick heat of July—and I figured it was because he didn't have a place safe enough to hang it. From there it was easy to figure that everything he owned was in its pockets. But I never knew how tough his life might be. It never showed. It never marked him. Nothing cut the spirit of his grin when he saw you coming half a block away, or stalled that ready laugh, or slowed that Johnny Appleseed stride, not even the unforgiving January winds that howled down the long canyons of the Avenues. It was a rare day when I didn't run into him or hear him holler from across the street. I told him once if he ever needed help to ask me. He looked surprised and then curious. I never brought it up again.

I only saw him twice without his hallmark grin. The first was the day Tom Carvel died. He took it hard. The second was a Monday three years into our street-bound friendship. It was hot. One of those days when the year stagnates in the backwash of August. He couldn't look at me. I'd never seen him evasive. I asked what was up. He asked shyly if I remembered telling him to ask me if he needed help. I went into my pocket. I had a five, a ten, two singles. I took the ten and held it out. He looked at it horrified and pushed my hand back.

"No, no, man!" he said. "Just those!"

"Two bucks? You sure?"

"Yeah! Just till Thursday!"

For the next two days I didn't see him. Early on Thursday I had to go out to Jersey. I got back to Penn Station after three and caught a cab home. Coming down Lex, the cabbie waited for an Indian man to cross the street, then cut off his trailing wife to nudge the big Caprice around the corner. Down the street I saw Jimmy in front of my building. When the cab stopped, he came up to the door, then backed off and looked away while I paid for the ride. He looked so happy to see me I was scared his grin would bust his face. He proudly held out two bucks. He'd rolled them up like a handmade cigarette.

"You been waiting?" I said.

"Naw, not waiting, just in the neighborhood, you know?"

He kept moving back and forth, still eager, like things weren't settled all the way. I told him thanks. He told me I was welcome. I stood there holding the money. I didn't want to put it in my pocket in front of him.

"Aren't you gonna spend it?" he said. "Get yourself a beer?"

I caught on. He'd gone since Monday thinking that by borrowing it, he'd deprived me of spending it. The debt wouldn't be fully paid until I broke the thirst he'd imposed on me.

"Sure," I said. "Let's go."

He shook his head and shied away. "Naw. I don't drink. But I know you been waiting to have one."

We headed for a place on the far corner of Third, a new joint, all glass along its two sidewalk walls. I went in and took a stool at the empty afternoon bar and ordered a Rolling Rock. He stayed outside, patrolling back and forth along the windows, looking in every few seconds. I held the bottle up. His grin broke out. He waved and kept patrolling. Halfway through the bottle he was satisfied. He cupped his eyes and looked inside a final time, over the heads of a startled couple at a window table, grinned and waved again, then turned and crossed back over Third, his debt paid, his world right again, his overcoat sailing on the heat of that August afternoon.

A few years ago I built a replica 1957 Porsche Speedster and entered a world of lunatic folks who built street-legal replicas of everything from pre-war sports cars to slick malevolent Le Mans racers. The most popular car was probably the Shelby Cobra. A beautiful American sports car with enough room under the hood for the biggest and meanest V8 you had the guts to try to handle. It could be called the Harley of the carbuilding hobby.

Back then the Cobra guys held the annual London Cobra Show. For me it was arguably the best event of this hobby. Two to three hundred Cobras converged on the Ohio town of London for a long weekend of parades, autocrosses, cruises, barbecues. Our hobby's rational answer to Sturgis. What gave it the heart that made it my personal favorite were the charity burnout rides the guys gave spectators—young and old alike—down Main Street. Zero to ninety in the fire and thunder and smoke of a couple of blocks. You could see it in their faces that their lives would never be the same. There was nothing like a Cobra. I always think of a hundred people I'd like to buy that ride for. My kids. The young cheerful disabled guy who helps me pull cardboard out of my car at the recycling place. Every girl in high school who passed me up for a guy whose idea of a thrill these days is a spaghetti breakfast at a laundromat. People I'd like to mend long-broken fences with.

And a street guy named Jimmy I last saw 30 years ago. I can't imagine that the trajectory of his life has altered much. He could easily still be there, on 30th Street, his dreads veined with silver, his grin tempered some by that relentlessly grim city, still keeping the neighborhood honest the way he did for me. A ride in a Cobra would scare him a million times more than the ten dollar bill he wouldn't take. But man would I like to buy him one while I hold his overcoat for him.

ZIMMER

MAX

•

•

•

•
•

•

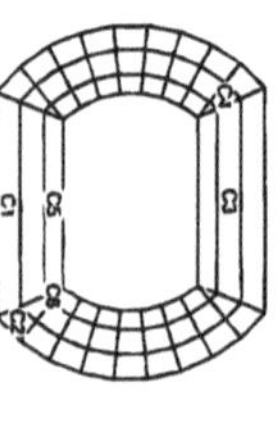

•

WHEN THERE IS

When there is a can of happy in the spring
and nothing winter says can make it glass

When there is a mug of joyful in the swing
and nothing homer does will let it pass

When there is a box of gladness in the ping
of tennis balls colliding in the grass

When there is a kindness glowing on the wing
and nothing kiss can do to wake a lass

When there is a crayon purple as the thing
you love to warm without your sister's gas

When there is an empty bucket full of sing
without the way you sip your sassafras

When there is a plate of glee done a la king
that never has to make you think of class

When there is a sack of lucky on the fling
and nothing sad will make it hard as brass

MAX

When there is a crate of smiles I could bring
without you have to lose your love for sass

Then there is

in the very gladness of the women lowing
when the bell for mass will ring

without your arms in ashes
in the promised smile of spring

the simple word for me.

UTAH DIED FOR YOUR SINS

You might have heard, somewhere in October, this way to hunt deer: take a double-edged razor blade, embed one edge in a salt block and leave the other edge in the air, and place the block on a deer trail. A deer comes out of the hills on its way to water after sunset and begins to lick the block. The first lick slices its tongue. As it continues to run its tongue across the block, the deer begins to get the better taste of licking its own blood with the salt. The animal will stand over the block and lick at the blade until it bleeds itself to death.

This method, you are told, has some advantage over the killing of a deer with a rifle. First of all, the traditional hunt has as a part of itself a chase. When a deer is shot at the end of such a chase, its muscles are pumped full of blood. This gives the meat too rough, almost too alive a taste. The blood, cooked in the meat, creates indigestion in some people. There is an unpalatable sense of thickness about it. On the other hand, when a deer licks at a razor blade in a block of salt, licks the salt away from around the blade so that the blade rises higher into the flesh, the animal is calm. There is a minimal flow of blood through its muscles. It has probably just eaten; its blood is concentrated in the inedible organs around its stomach. And it will die only after the heart has pumped the muscles and the organs out, only after the meat has been bled thoroughly by the tongue. Venison is a wild meat. Blood carries the taste of bark and harsh grass. The absence of blood in the meat minimizes this wild aspect of its flavor.

You would further have heard that, as the trend is away from a hunter developing his sense of aim at a target range, a gunshot from a modern rifle is designed to kill or adequately maim a deer without regard to where it enters the animal. Whoever you heard this from has the story of having seen three legs amputated from a deer in a forest with a solitary shot. A complaint against a gunshot is that it inevitably ruins, in its method of mushrooming into a round plow, a substantial portion of the edible flesh. A razor blade in a block of salt costs only the tongue. It does not shred or hack at anything else. Some people prefer to eat tongue; there is no argument with them; let them carry their rifles after a deer, and aim, when they can, away from the head.

And, at last, there is a humane and pastoral element to a deer that is dead as if it had slept there, after filling its belly with blood that will not be digested. Such a deer is easier to butcher than a deer that has been, say, gutshot. A gutshot deer has lost the heterogeneity of its organs; there is nothing to be learned about how the human body functions in the butchering of a gutshot deer.

So there are razor blades that never shave an armpit or a leg or a face. There are razor blades that never graze the skin; razor blades that, instead, stand in wait for animals that graze on high and slanted meadows. There are razor blades that never slice an apple on Halloween, although you read about those apples in October, at breakfast, already shaved for the day.

Consider this. If you had an automobile in 1959, and held your cigarette in the palm of your hand at night at a hamburger drive-in and looked out at the street, you would not be bored with yourself or with your automobile. Nor, here in October, on the outskirts of a Utah town, would you have heard of alloy wheels. You would have a friend with a 1940 Ford; he would have it thoroughly cherried out. Your 1951 Olds would look to you as though a hundred relatives had aged it whenever the Ford is around. You would choose, as a consequence, to customize your Olds. This is how you do it.

Appletons are shells that resemble spotlights. They attach to the posts of the windshield, and have the shape of small, brilliant warheads on your fenders. You purchase a pair from Western Auto. You make, from quarter-inch boilerplate, a set of shackles to bolt into the A-frames behind your wheels, and lower the front of your Olds by four inches. Your work runs you into November and, to avoid having your hands become clumsy with the cold air, you work now in your father's garage. You dismantle the exhaust system, and rebuild it with glasspack mufflers and scavenger pipes, two or four flared tubes that hang out under your axle. You remove all the trim from the body, remove the hood ornament, remove the trunk ornament, and push putty into the resultant holes. You flush the putty with the contour of the body using a sanding block; you paint your Olds with either metalflake or fishscale mixed into a color from the spectrum of Fuller automotive paints. Or you paint it candy apple red. You hang a tie or your high school tassel on the rearview mirror. You fix a hula dancer that has a pair of eyehooks for a pelvis, or a dog with imitation ruby eyes that are wired to your brakelights, on the deck in the rear window.

There is an old round refrigerator in your father's garage. Random cans of Olympia and Coors rattle on the shelves when you smack the refrigerator door shut, and you have a habit, now, of looking out the window at the asphalt as you drink half the can. If you took an Olympia, you scratch the paper label in half, and look at the dots on the back. There are from one two four of them, in a short brown row.

One dot is to find her. Two are to find her and feel her. Three are to do these, and fuck her, and with four dots you get to forget her. You replace your rockerarm covers and air cleaner with chrome accessories, and tap a wolf whistle you ordered from J.C. Whitney into the intake manifold, and force the wire that controls the whistle through the firewall and into the passenger compartment. You weld a row of razor blades inside the lip of the hood. Your customary luck with dots is two.

And last you have the spinner hubcaps. They are round pressed plates as all hubcaps are; they have two raised bars that cross one another and span the plate. They are four thick spokes that knife out from the center of the hubcap in four directions. You press the spinners into the wheelrims because alloy wheels have not occurred yet at the accessory shops. Also, your Olds is used; you bought it when it was seven years old, with the spots worn where you would not have worn them, with crumbs and french fries that are rough on your fingertips when you push your hands into the fat cloth crack between the bench and the backrest. And you look across the black metal dashboard and find it laced with the transparent coronas of drinks that perhaps are seven years old as well; some of the stains are indelible, rings of microscopic blisters under the surface of the paint, and the windshield there ahead of you has been starred in four places by rocks. The splines of the stars are the edges of split glass, and they catch the sunset and make fiery spears of it when you yaw the Olds back and forth along a canyon road. The front left wheel sets a steady tremor at 65 miles an hour which the Olds amplifies with rattles you think it has always had.

So you resent that your Olds has a history without you. You hear that it belonged to a basketball coach at a local high school, and so you come to avoid that neighborhood. You have modified it to avoid these discomforts of its past, rather than joined your history with it, and this is no ordinary luck.

Rather, this is November. You sit with your date in your automobile much as you would sit with her in a restaurant: together, on one half of the booth, you both look at the half where you chose not to sit, you both look at the windshield. On your table, you look at the same coronas of those unknown drinks as on your dashboard. You, this is more obscure to you now; she is who she is because you have chosen her to sit in your customized Olds, spinners and all. She is not opposite you, nor have you thought of her as opposite you, never had her at a kitchen table. She knows the Olds is yours for what she wants. She shaves her legs with her father's safety razor, she tells you, as high as her knees. You hear this, you look at your car keys, you look at your radio, you look at her; the Olds is no longer yours. She lets your blood, not hers, when you feel the hot Kotex in her crotch. At dawn, if you have a rooster in your rear window, its crow will have the sound of a woman with a knife in her throat, sobbing.

But with the advent of alloy wheels, the spinner is a style of hubcap that has been defunct, now, for longer than you can recollect, except in remote areas of Utah, where alloy wheels are still unheard of. There the accessory shops still carry spinners. There, you can look at a 1940 Ford with its spinners twisting the lights, at midnight, into cellophane-spangled toothpicks, and have three probabilities occur to you: The first, that the rear axle is locked, so that the rear wheels never deviate from one another in their rate of revolution, so that rubber is sloughed off whenever the Ford rounds a curve. The second, that its spinners will rotate on who knows whose automobile in another month, perhaps yours. And the third, that your next hamburger will be stabbed with that kind of toothpick, when you raise it on that kind of night to your teeth in a crowd of high school kids.

The second probability occurs to you because spinners are as easy as silverware to steal. You wrap your hands around the spokes, and you transact four sharp yanks with Midnight Auto. To stall you, your friend has installed hubcap locks that use the valve stem as their anchor. These are heavy and complicated knobs that would require you to rebalance your wheels, as he has; you would have to steal his wheel weights as well. Or he has etched his name into a hidden place

on the back, and let it be spread that his spinners are marked and registered. Or he has taken the law into his own hands. The spokes of his spinners, from the rear, are hollow. He has pushed putty into the spokes from the rear. He has cut a number of double-edged razor blades halfway down into the putty. He has left you with your fingers pointing off your hands in eight directions at once. Each finger is a castanet. Each direction is an escape route.

As a result, your fingers only rattle now, when your hands try to imitate how they once could cup a cigarette up against your palm. You only have the act as a memory, and to reinvigorate what you remember, you walk while you are hunting onto a dirt road in an autumn blizzard and try to hold handfuls of mud.

To hunt, to steal, to masturbate are to yearn to be self-held, to be hermaphroditic. They have been rewarded, in older cultures, by amputating the hands at the wrists. Look who you are, without your hands. You hide in the Olds. You run the Olds out to show how your

spinners pluck at the neon curlicues up and down the street. You ask where hamburgers are sold in sacks. Look what you could do.

And once you are without hands, a friend delivers a candle she has molded, out of paraffin and aluminum foil, into the shape of a hexagonal nut. You catch yourself at the thought of wrenches. You resent mementos and medals and poorly chosen presents. You make the effort to type a letter to her; you read the letter aloud, and your mouth aches.

It has been my experience, you read, with the candle you gave me, that aluminum foil does not burn. Therefore, your candle has become an ashtray. Imagine how long it will take a candle to burn away because of the cigarettes I happen to stub out in the wax and aluminum foil around its wick. Keep your father's razor sharp, and don't come around here hairy at the knees.

But here you are let off the hook; here you hit four dots. The name at the end of the letter is not yours. It is Seymour Utah. Suppose he has hands. He, then, is the friend with the 1940 Ford. Now, more than thirty years old, he has a motorcycle also, a 360 Bultaco, manufactured for riding in the hills, a dirt bike ready to ride from the factory. He has added the equipment to enable himself to ride it on the street as well.

One afternoon he rides it to the Ratskeller for an eight-inch venison pizza. The Ratskeller has venison pizza available during the deerhunt in October. Utah likes to leave his helmet with his bike, and he has already had two helmets stolen. More interested, still, in punishment than in prevention, he has formed a piece of steel into a band that fits behind the padded headband in his helmet, and has welded seventeen razor blades around the interior of the band. He inserts the band into his helmet whenever he parks the bike. If a thief has no knowledge of it, the band would treat his head the way a Vegematic would. Utah keeps the headband in the compartment beneath his seat when he rides the Bultaco. He looks over the counter, where the cook runs a razorsharp handheld wheel across the pizza four times, without having it fall apart. Against a wall, at a table the size of his lap, Utah eats the pizza with his hands, clearheaded enough for anybody, clearheaded enough to recall the last time he took a deer out of the hills himself.

It was two years ago. It was four miles off the highway, off a dirt spur that would lead to Cedar Fork, along a deer trail. The deer had been in motion, in the air, and its legs had folded around its stomach as it fell. It had been gutshot. It began to blizzard as Utah ran the slurry of the deer's guts out onto the sparse snow. He set it on its hooves and held it with his knees. This let him reach around to the chest from the back and spread the ribcage open. Staggering, the animal in his arms, he lifted it and fit it backward over the Bultaco. He didn't want another hunter to think he was riding a live deer; he didn't want another hunter thinking he could shoot it out from under him. When he had it seated right, its ribcage held the gas tank, its rear legs dangled out over the handlebars, and its head would swing in the mud of the knobbed rear tire. He rode the deer and the bike, like a child on a mechanized animal, the four miles of the slippery trail back to the highway. He was covered with mud. Mud covered him and the deer in a communal hide. Mud sloughed out of its ribcage when he pulled the deer off the Bultaco.

He had long ago unlocked the rear axle of the Ford. Parked on the shoulder where the mud road rose to the highway, it was no more now than an old automobile, with a rack he had bought for the Bultaco hung off the rear bumper. He pulled the mud out of the deer and pushed the mud off his arms. He looked up the highway to where the mud ran into the sky. The animal was folded into the trunk and driven the thirty miles to Kearns where Utah lived. The wipers did not work in the blizzard.

A razor blade is honed to enough of an edge that the first recognition of having been cut is not a result of pain. After he left the Ratskeller, Utah was first aware of what he had forgotten to do, and had done, when he thought that it was too red and too early in the afternoon for a sunset. He was amazed at the beauty, first of all, of what he had thought was a sunset. The beat of the Bultaco on the highway became hard to distinguish from the taste of the pizza. Both perceptions ran down his throat. He headed his dirt bike west on the Bingham highway. The helmet covered his face completely, except for those regions of his face where he had to shave. The wind dried the blood there, as it ran down the slant of his cheeks one layer after another, like thin red frosting on his whiskers. He pushed the helmet off his head while he rode. He began to look for a half-familiar dirt road toward Cedar Fork. His hand reached out to turn the bright ring of the rearview mirror up until he could look at his face. The mirror shook from the resonance of the engine. In the mirror his head shook. For a moment, while his hand worked at the final adjustment of the mirror, and before he turned it rapidly downward again, his hand held this pocketsized, shaking portrait of himself: a huge rotting tomato in the wind, or a heart that stood and oozed blood onto his shoulders. He was most astonished at how calm his hands were on the handlegrips, at how logical it was to have a tachometer, a gray gasoline tank, and the gray rumbling smudge of the highway all between his knees. It all worked. It all came together. He was an extrapolation of all this logic. And there was the road toward Cedar Fork. He turned off the highway and onto the dirt road. He could feel himself sweat more than he could feel himself bleed. As the Bultaco dropped off the highway, as he shifted it down, his left hand pulled and released the clutch lever and his right hand twisted the accelerator grip as calmly as paper gloves that have just been tossed onto a fire, that always look, for a moment, before they tremble and crack apart at their kindling temperature, as though they are there to calm the flames. His left shoe worked the notches of the gearshift pedal.

The road hurried him up toward the cedar. He scratched the blood from his eyes. The mirror struck him now as a circular, bouncing postcard of the country he had come across, the country he was leaving orange with October dust. He ignored the notion of sending the postcard anywhere. It would not hold still enough to sign, he thought; besides, he liked postcards of wildlife; at a Union 76 truckstop, he had bought eleven postcards of a jackelope once, depicted in a butchered taxidermist's trick as a jackrabbit with the antlers of a Wyoming antelope, and had mailed four of them. One had come to your address. Hoping to put an animal on the mirror, he turned the Bultaco onto a deer trail. He followed his hands. All he knew about was how thirsty he was, after the pizza, and how a deer trail, if it did not lead to water, would go on into the hills until it did lead to water. Utah had heard this from an old deerhunter. What he did not know was that it had been said to him to keep him out of the way. How many miles is uncertain when, eventually, he laid his head in the trail, and the Bultaco, held at full throttle, scrambled out from under him like

Like. This is complicated. Like a half-eaten grasshopper. Like a spider bereft of its legs on one side. Like a jackrabbit speared to the earth. Or like a rattlesnake, broken almost in half by a stone, its two halves thrashing, as though this would make sense to it of its wound.

Then here is this. Does a rattlesnake coil or uncoil from such a wound. Does it rattle. Do its two halves coil and uncoil simultaneously, or, one half coiling, the other uncoiling from the node originated by the stone, in syncopation. The hardship here is that animals and insects abound. You think of your own. Remember only: it has to do with nodes. You take the node of something and you relocate the node. The node of the Bultaco, about which all else revolves, is the naugahyde seat. The node of the human is the crotch. The node of the razor blade is the place where you hold it. You can make the seat the engine. You can make the crotch the hand. And you can make the place where you hold the razor blade the part of the blade that will not let you hold it.

Leftovers Utah had not known:

That alloy wheels had lately come on the market there in town for motorcycles too. That the node of an animal is its tongue. Nor that a deer, having drunk enough of its own blood, will become a carnivorous animal, and for how long is conjectural.

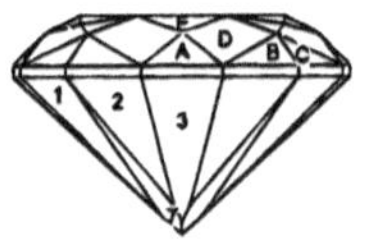
E
A D B C
1 2 3

ASKING FOR NOTHING

Where will you be
when the wind stops
and the long sleeves
of your frail dress
no longer sail you
through the afternoon?

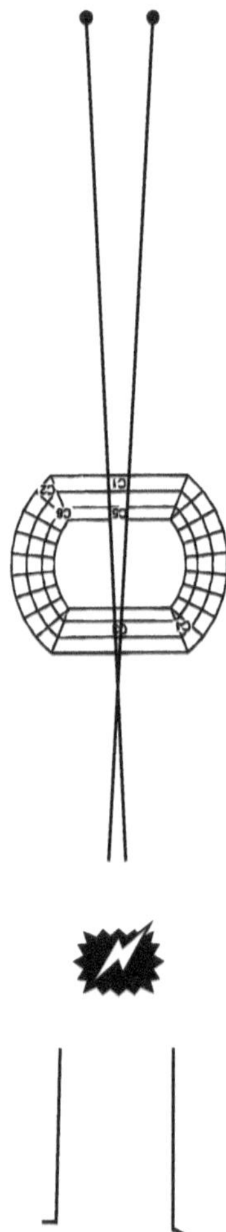

THE MAGIC RADIO

Back in school I owned a 1953 Buick Roadmaster Riviera for a while. I bought it off a guy who restored vintage cars. He'd bought more cars than he could handle and needed to unload a few. The big Buick caught my interest because a similar Buick—a 1953 economy model with the same white on green paint scheme—was the first car my dad bought for his family. I thought that owning and driving one would give me some clue into our relationship. I could never do much to please him except grow up and move out. Too wild. Too much trouble. Maybe an old Buick would help. I wasn't planning on owning it for long. I just wanted it long enough to help me explain my dad.

The Riviera was tired. Its paint was oxidized to a dull turquoise and gone in places to where you could see the underlying primer. It had power windows that worked on hydraulic cylinders too worn out to hold fluid. You had to raise and lower the windows manually by pulling them up and pushing them down. Even then they would only stay halfway up. The red leather bench was split and torn along its stitches. But the car was clean. No rust. No bondo. Free of dents.

The big engine ran well. I don't remember the odometer reading but I do recall being impressed by the low mileage. The car had apparently spent part of its lifetime in storage. No oil or water leaks. No exhaust leaks. The tires showed the beginning spiderweb lines of dry rot in the sidewalls. No problem. New tires. The power steering didn't squeal. No excess lag in the Dynaflow transmission.

It was a lazy driver's car. It was huge. You rode high. Out the windshield was the longest hood I'd ever looked down the length of. Its soft shocks would let a bump in the road echo a few times. There was serious roll when you turned a corner. Serious pitch if you hit the brakes too hard. It wasn't that I was lazy. It just needed to be driven in a lazy kind of way.

The dashboard was a shameless expression of 1950s automotive art. The centerpiece was the radio with its big chrome speaker grill.

It wasn't long before I discovered a button on the left side of the floor that looked a lot like a second dimmer switch. It didn't seem to do anything when I stepped on it. Then, one day out driving, singing along on "It's too Late" with Carole King on the radio, my left foot jumping, it happened. My foot hit that button. Bam. All of a sudden Carole King and her piano were gone—lost to some guy talking about traffic. I gave the button another pop. Sure enough. Bam. Next station. Bam. Classical. Bam. Jazz. Bam. Vietnam. When it got to the far end of the dial it came back to the beginning. I was amazed. Today it's probably tough to find a car whose radio doesn't have a seek switch. Back then I'd never heard of anything like it.

And this is where the story starts.

This was back when hitchhiking was safe and popular. I started picking up every hitchhiker I came across. I always had the radio going. I'd mastered the button so that the only thing that visibly moved was the toe of my left shoe in the dark of the footwell. I'd ask where they were headed. Start a conversation. A lot of them wanted to know about the car. Thought it was cool. Somewhere along the way I'd look at the radio, say "Change," and pop that button. Some of them were too self-absorbed to notice at first. I'd have to do it two or three more times before I had their attention.

"Wait a minute. What'd you just do?"

"What?"

"You said 'change' and the radio changed stations."

Sometimes they'd sit there wide-eyed like they'd seen a miracle. Sometimes they'd get scared. Sometimes they'd turn and look out the window and not say a word. Sometimes they'd get belligerent. Like I was messing with them. But here's how it would usually go.

"Yeah. I did."

"How?"

"There's a voice actuator behind the grill there."

"What's a voice actuator?"

"A gizmo that hears a command and activates something," I'd say. And then, if they were curious I'd tell them that during the Korean war the army had made a lot of them and never used them. So they struck a deal with Buick. If Buick stopped using some rare metal and gave it to the army for its electronic systems, they'd give Buick all these voice actuators they didn't need. Sometimes I'd say navy. The navy needed the metal for its sonar systems. I'd change the metal too.

"Wow. Do it again."

"Change."

"Man. That's amazing."

"Wanna try it?"

"Sure."

"Go ahead."

"Change."

Nothing would happen. I needed to see them work for it.

"It's old. It only hears a couple of pitches. Lower your voice a little and try it.

"Change."

Nothing would happen. I needed to get my money's worth.

"That's a little too low. Bring it up just a bit."

They'd wet their lips. Sit up. Look at the speaker grill.

"Change."

Depending on how they'd committed themselves, or how much fun I could have with them, I'd keep it going.

"Here. Listen carefully to my pitch. Change."

They'd stare at the radio as the dial moved a station over.

"Change."

It always depended. Sometimes they'd perfectly match my pitch. Sometimes I'd see them start to lose interest. And I'd reward them by punching the button. Or I wouldn't. But when I did, this was usually what would happen.

"Oh my god. It worked."

"It did. Congratulations."

That was when they'd sometimes slide to the middle of the bench, lean forward, and put their face right up to the speaker grill.

"Change. Change. Change. Change. Change." On and on. Every third or fourth time I'd reward them. Others, mostly guys, would be happy with getting it once, and sit back smug as cats and proud as peacocks.

I felt like a king. I felt like a puppetmaster. Sometimes I felt satanic. Like my Buick and I could rule the world.

The obvious question is whether I ever let them in on the joke. The answer? Not once. I wanted word to spread about this guy whose Buick had a voice actuated radio. I wanted the story told about this deal the army or navy made with Buick.

The car never did help me explain my dad. Maybe because he kept his radio tuned to a classical music station and wouldn't change it for anyone. Maybe there wasn't a button on his floor. Maybe I could have picked him up and played the joke on him. But I never saw him on the side of the road with his thumb up in the air.

•

•

•

ZIMMER

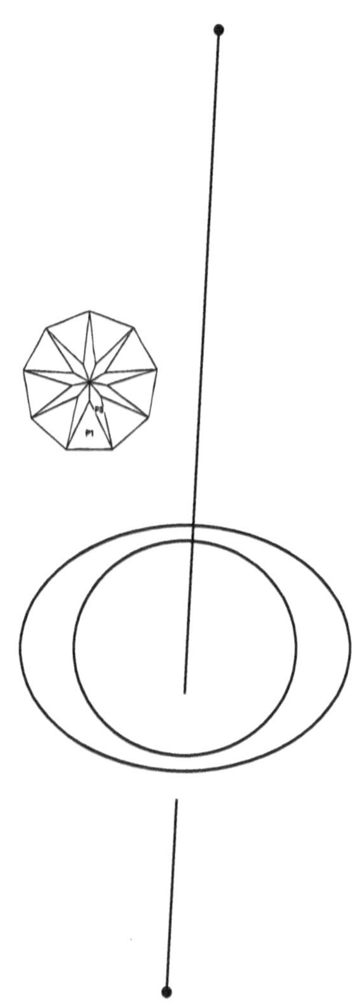

NEWLY WED

When you pick her up at the hospital after work, in the light blue Volkswagen that still shows the phantoms of the wedding graffiti when it rains, you can smell the day's disinfectant in her green uniform. When you take her head and put your mouth on the skin behind her ear, you can smell the disinfectant deep in her blond hair, and feel the wet heat off the back of her neck. When she rests her hand on the thigh of your levis you can feel the heat again. She doesn't talk when you slip a right through the red light at South Temple and glance across at her to see points of sweat on the flares of her nostrils. You have nothing to say when she reaches down below the dash to untie her hospital shoes and her hair cascades across her flushed face. When you get her home and her clothes come off, you can see the welt the elastic band of her pantyhose has left like the scar of a thin bloodsucking worm around her waist, the way her pubic hair has been smashed as flat as winter grass against the field it makes below her belly, the way her breasts look molded and her nipples crushed by the cups of her bra when she shakes the straps off her arms. When you drop your levis you can see the way your t-shirt goes from gray to white at the line where your belt rode. When you pull its neck off your face, you can smell, on your slick raw fingers, the metal and grease from the cutters and rivet gun you've used that day to nail sheets of quivering tin to the rafters of four more mobile homes. You think, right then, that maybe you should take a shower first. Or wash your hands. Or wait for the welt to fade. Or the disinfectant to leave her hair. Or her nipples and pubic hair to revive from the rigging of her underwear. Check the mail. Play with the kitten. Let the day fall back to where the two of you won't feel like you're doing this on the living room linoleum of a half built trailer house or on the tile floor of a hospital closet. Open this gift you both got married for with the reverence your wedding guests would hope to see you exercise. But here you are. Here where the engine of your Volkswagen still ticks and pings with heat out in the parking lot. Here where she can see that your feet are welted with the stitches left in them by the laces and the eyelets of your work boots. Here where the tuna fish sandwich you ate out of your lunchbox has left the feel of old newspaper on your unbrushed teeth. Here where she can feel how your knees are crabbed from kneeling on the scaffold to get the rivets into the tin up under the overhang of the roof. Here where her sweat takes the afternoon sun from the room's one window and makes her waiting body gleam where she's thrown herself across the crocheted bedspread neither of you can take the time to tear away. Here you are, as pitiless as jackals among your wedding gifts, as ruthless as crows for what was always there.

•

•

Here in this bedroom, among the Early American chest and
dresser and matching nightstands you sold your Firebird
for a month ago, her sweat is your sweat. On the Beautyrest
mattress and box spring with the headboard still on lay-
away, her eyes are your eyes. Her arms your arms. Your levis
and t-shirt her uniform. You've done your time. Sent thank
you notes to the friends and relatives who hoped you could
keep this decent. Take each other here, now, in this instant
where the evidence of what you are is new enough to make
you sob. On the tile floor of the janitor's closet, while the
rubber wheels of a gurney roll past outside the door, her
surgical assistant's hands reach deep enough into your back
to drive their claws into your stomach. On the linoleum
floor of the half-built trailer house, while rivets are punched
through the tin and work boots idle back and forth along
the scaffold out the window, your roofer's fangs reach deep

enough into her throat to draw blood from her lungs. Here you are. Unclean and savage and stinking among your gifts. In the afterwork rush hour heat in the airless bedroom of this rented second floor apartment. The beasts that your wedding has finally let you make of one another. Her cry your cry. Your flesh her flesh. A priest gave you this right. A priest gave you this right.

TIME WAITS

I remember back to when I thought I was infinite. It wasn't that long ago. Time—its movement—meant nothing to me. I had truckloads of it. Reservoirs up in the mountains of my mind. More than I'd use up in a lifetime. I alternated that heretic belief with the equally specious theory that if I sat still, or just stood there, or went to sleep, time stopped too. It would wait for me. It wouldn't start off again until I started doing something. And then it paced itself depending on what I was doing. Humping furniture out of someone's house into the back of a Mayflower truck? Time flew like a hummingbird. Making a run from Salt Lake to Portland? Time crawled behind the picture window of a windshield like it was going eight hundred miles in granny gear. These days I can't stand to watch the timer on my microwave. Want to watch your life go by? Those are real seconds counting off while you stand there.

And remembering Mayflower reminds me of the summer a mover named Tim and I were dispatched to move a load from Salt Lake to Los Angeles, where we picked up another load for a family moving to Phoenix, and a Rolling Stones song I heard for the first time on that move.

The family we were moving to Phoenix had a little girl who had a small aquarium with a couple of goldfish. We told her dad we could only take the aquarium empty. It was up to him to tell his daughter. She started crying. I saved the day. I suggested she put her goldfish in a Mason jar. We'd put the jar on the dashboard so her goldfish would have a nice view of the scenery. The family left. We finished loading and headed out. This was July. Phoenix was a straight west-to-east shot across seven hours of desert on Interstate 10. The truck's AC was out so we rode with the windows open and our teeshirts off. Time slowed to a pace that never let us reach that distant silver oasis on the horizon We stopped halfway at a place called Desert Center. I'd never seen a place with wall-to-wall coolers. I paid for water for the first time in my life. Back in the truck we switched drivers. I took the wheel. We were barely on the interstate again when Tim said, "Oh Jesus." He was looking at the dashboard. In the Mason jar, in the sun, one goldfish had exploded. The other one was starting to open up. After we rode out the panic we decided we'd just get replacements in Phoenix. Tim burned his hands taking the top off the jar and dumping it out the window.

"We can look around for a goldfish store in the morning before we go unload."

"No," I said. "I promised her we'd bring them by tonight."

We lumbered that semi around Phoenix for maybe an hour looking for a goldfish place before we stumbled across a K-Mart. Did K-Mart sell goldfish? We didn't know. But we got inside and found our answer. A wall of aquariums held maybe ten thousand goldfish. All colors. All sizes. All shapes. All ethnicities. Like goldfish from every country in the world.

"Remember what they looked like?"

"They weren't very big. I remember that."

"I should of saved them," said Tim.

For a minute we both just looked at the empty Mason jar he was holding.

"I got it," I said.

"What?"

"Let's get a couple of the darker ones. Tell her they picked up a tan coming across the desert."

"That's what you call a tan," said Tim.

"Then you think of something."

"A tan's good."

With new goldfish, fresh free water, some flakes of food in the Mason jar, we found the family's house. The little girl came running out before we'd even stopped the truck along the curb. Her dad trailed out behind her. By then, in the gathering dusk, she'd already seen the goldfish, and was already bawling her eyes out. We hadn't even had time to lie to her.

"What's wrong. Angel?" her dad said.

"They're not Sammy and Charley!" she cried. "I don't know who they are!"

Her dad looked at me. "What happened?"

"The AC went out on the truck," I said. "It was working when we left Los Angeles." It was easier to lie to her dad than to her. "Halfway across the desert it just quit. It was the heat." Then I said, "I'm sorry."

"It'll be okay, Angel. You can name them."

"I don't want them!"

Her dad looked at me. He was as helpless as I was.

"Any way we can make it up to you?" I asked. "We could unload tonight. You'd have your beds."

"You'd do that?"

We did that. Set up all the furniture in the house including the empty aquarium. Dropped all the boxes in the right rooms. We got out of there around eleven. By then, the little girl's mom had calmed her down, talked her into adopting her surrogate goldfish, and hooked up the aquarium. We headed north. We'd polished off the baloney sandwiches her mom had made for us before we were out of Phoenix. The windows were open to the cool night air and the smell of orange. After its slow death crawl across the desert, the empty trailer rattled and banged, but the ships painted on its sides were under full sail and flew us through the night back to Salt Lake in time for a breakfast of waffles and eggs at Denny's.

That Stones song? It came on the truck radio somewhere along the way home. It was called Time Waits for No One. "Time waits for no one," Jagger belts out, "and it won't wait for me." And at the end, guest guitarist Mick Taylor goes into a haunting solo I occasionally have Alexa play, especially when time keeps moving no matter how still I stand there watching that timer. No, Jagger, time does wait. Take a look at your buddy Keith over there.

HAVING LEFT HOME TWICE

When I shoot my brother
this is how things play out:
the bullet goes through his cheek
he catches it with his teeth
and you, father,
come to the porch to tell me
what my brother
can't free himself to say.

That he didn't mean
to walk around
your house that way. That
he didn't mean
to lay claim to his pick
of your belongings
to take with him after you
yourself were dead. You
are emphatic, father,
when you say
that he did it only
at his mother's invitation.

Emphatic when you say
that the invitation now

is open to me. Standing
where your well-cut grass
meets the curb
of your clean street
I watch my brother
stand beside you
the bullet still in his teeth
the victory he shares
with his mother over you
clenched in his obscene smile.

Inside your house
like things for sale
in a gift shop
the choicest of your souvenirs
collector plates
figurines
and other keepsakes
gathered in your lifetime
can be overturned
for the rest of us
to see small labels
bearing his first name.

It was my house too.
It is my turn now. Father,
I can tell you
my brother will not die
of a bullethole in his cheek.
He will outlive
what you hope for him.
And he will be here
once you are in the ground

his black wheelbarrow open
like the suitcase
you once threw after me
having asked me to leave
your house.

If I were not your son
if I could call you
by your own first name
then you and I would see
that there is nothing
we need to leave behind.
Even this rifle
which I hold now
like a cane for a wounded leg
even this rifle
would go to him.

TOWN WITHOUT PITY

If you look closely you'll see it. Faint at first—but look long enough and it sharpens and starts to take on form and detail and come to life. It isn't much of a life. It doesn't go anywhere or live for very long. But while it does, it's a spectacular thing to behold. The color and light it gives off are amazing. For a moment, before it dies, it briefly forms a miniature but exact replica of the planet Earth, hovering above the teaspoon it came from. Then it implodes in another burst of light and color.

"Jesus."

"So you saw that."

"It's what astronauts get to see."

"It's populated too."

"No."

"It is. But you'd need an electron microscope to see the people."

"What happens to them?"

"At the end? They get cremated, I guess. But they always come back the next time you do it."

"Like being resurrected?"

"Yeah. Or reincarnated."

The beginning and end of the world. In a teaspoon. I was introduced to it by a guy who worked at one of the power plants I worked for too when I came East. His name was John. The plant was being repowered from old coal-fired steam generators to combustion turbine generators capable of burning both oil and gas. He was shift supervisor He's retired now, and moved away without leaving a number or new address, and he never told me what it was. He just showed it to me in his office once. It was a gray powder. He had a little jar of it. He took out a teaspoon and leveled it off with a knife. He lightly breathed on it. And that's how it got started.

The only drawback was the smell. I've never smelled anything so foul. But John said you can't hold your nose or your breath. That kills it long before the show ends. You just had to live with it. The smell made its lifespan seem unbearably long. It left the teaspoon clean.

"Where'd you get it?"

"Does it matter?"

My dentist at the time collected jukeboxes. He also had a TV set mounted in the dropped ceiling of his office so that the screen was flush with the acoustic ceiling tiles. When he laid you back in his chair, the screen looked straight down on you, and you looked straight up at it. He had a collection of video tapes to choose from and would ask you what you'd like to watch. They were mostly old half-hour TV shows because his patients usually were only there that long. I just wanted to close my eyes and forget about a TV set hanging over my head. Especially a heavy old set with a picture tube for a screen. I never much trusted his mounting job. And I couldn't see myself watching Green Acres or The Rifleman while someone had their fingers in my mouth.

John was looking ahead to his retirement a few months down the road and sometimes talked about all the stuff he wanted to get rid of before he moved. One thing he mentioned was an old jukebox he had in his basement. He didn't know what to do with it.

"Does it work?" I asked.

"Last time I checked," he said.

"I might have a customer for you."

"Who? he asked.

"My dentist. He collects them."

"Your dentist collects jukeboxes?"

"Yeah. And he's got a TV set mounted in his ceiling."

John smiled and slowly shook his head.

"What?"

"Dentists," he said. "A strange breed. Have him call me."

Back home from the plant that day I called my dentist and gave him John's number. They worked out a deal on the phone. My dentist rented a pickup truck and asked if I could help him bring the jukebox home. We drove down to John's place in Linden. John played a couple of songs on it.

John looked me up and down.

"I don't know how you're going to get it out of the basement," he said. I can't help. Not with my back."

"So it's good I brought Mavis," my dentist said. "She's tough."

"Showgirl legs. Wrestler arms."

"What do you know," said John, smiling. "I had no idea."

They closed the deal and we humped it out of the basement and into the truck. We were ready to leave when John took me aside and handed me the little jar in a paper bag.

"I won't be needing this either," he said. "Want it?" I took it.

On the drive back, I told my dentist about the stuff John had shown me in his teaspoon, the stuff that rode now in a paper bag between my knees. How it came to life, lived briefly in a spectacular display

of color and light, and then died. How bad it smelled. I figured, being a dentist, he knew something about chemistry. But he had no idea. It doesn't sound legal, was all he said. Back at his house I helped him lug the machine down his basement stairs where his jukebox collection stood lined around the walls.

"Do they all work?" I asked.

"Pretty much," he said.

"Do you ever turn them on all at once?"

He looked at me like out of the two of us, I was the oddball, the one who mounted TV sets in ceilings.

"No," he said, like I should have known. "I'd need a dedicated generator to run them all at once." A generator, I thought. Now he's talking my language. He plugged his jukebox in and lit it up. "Name an old song," he said.

"Town Without Pity," I said.

"One of my favorites too," he said.

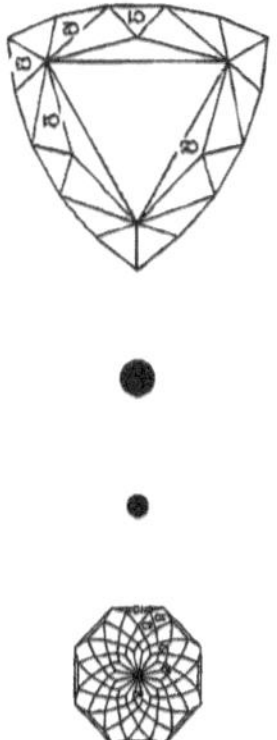

Because I was always on the move, I have a new dentist now, one with a regular ceiling. John's long gone. They've commissioned the repower project They've asked me back but I had to turn them down. I'd moved on. At home that night from helping my dentist out, I stuck a label on the jar, wrote Spot on it, the name of a dog I never had, and if anyone asked, I told them it held his ashes. Other than that, I only touch the jar on the Fourth of July, when I lock the door of the Airstream, draw the shades, kill the lights, take out a level teaspoon and breathe on it.

I still don't know what it is. How it does what it does. But I was raised—like many of us—in a church that taught me to beware of asking too many questions. Sometimes you had to accept things you didn't understand on faith. I agree. The answer could always destroy the child's magic that resides in the innocence of every question. So I don't ask. I just lock myself away in the Airstream and watch the world begin and end with a child's wonder all by myself while Alexa plays Town Without Pity.

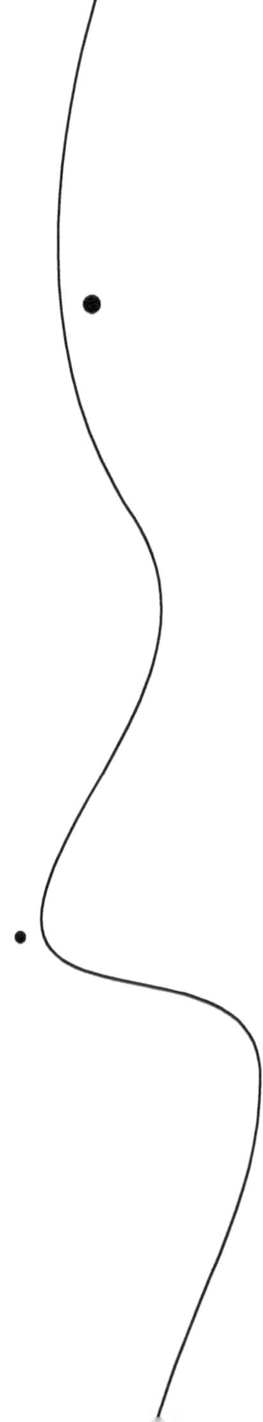

AMERICAN RIVER

I have learned that
the low horizon off in the distance through my window is the
Kittatinny Ridge. It marks the western edge of New Jersey and
the eastern edge of what we call America. Off its far side runs
the Delaware River

and beyond that
those towns of these United States Route 80 stitches together like
a necklace of flagstones. You chase America west. Pennsylvania.
Ohio. Indiana. Illinois. Iowa. The stones of the heartland all of us
have learned about.

and beyond that
the day you spend crossing Nebraska. The sunset you start to
chase across the final hundred miles of the panhandle as America
lifts you toward the Rockies. There is the night it takes you to get
across Wyoming.

then Utah. In that
last holdout of America before you cross the foreign shoreline of
Nevada is where I come from. Above this ridge out my window the
falling sun fulfills yet again the American metaphor of a sunset.
and beyond that

there is another
metaphor from where I come: a man lies working on his stomach
in his yard. With both his hands he gives shape to a small moat of
soil around the trunk of a rosebush. I see him swimming and smell
beyond the soil

the Great American
River that he swims
like all of us are taught
to swim.

WOLVES COME RUNNING

Fourteen soldiers from the Bolivian Army (Ejército Boliviano) knocked on the door to my Airstream this morning. They were after a guy named Desmond. Apparently, while I was away last week, he took the initiative to commandeer my mailing list and send out a wild story about Charlie Steen, Calcutta, a Moab restaurant, and a speedboat named The Flying Sharon he claimed I'd drawn for my best friend, a miner's daughter when I was a kid. The contingent of Bolivian soldiers was led by a lieutenant. He wanted to know where they could find Desmond. I couldn't help them beyond an outdated Facebook page and cell number. I couldn't even give them a last name because Desmond and I had taken a childhood oath to never share last names. And over the years we'd both respected it. I wanted to know why Bolivia was interested in him. They couldn't tell me except that it had to do with sheep. I offered them coffee. They asked if it was Bolivian. I told them no. It was French Roast. They left in peace. I wished them well.

I kind of wish it had gone that way. But the soldiers had a pack of Bolivian wolves in the caged bed of one of their pickup trucks. And Bolivian wolves—a brand of maned wolves—can smell a lie coming all the way from Omaha. They feed on lies. They're like piranhas when it comes to lies. So what I told the soldiers was the truth. That Desmond was my imaginary friend. One of many. I made him up years ago when I was writing for a car club. A kind of illusory reader, at times an alter ego, a guy I could make fun of, do what I wanted with. Sometimes, when I needed someone to tell me I was being stupid, he was a kind of personal Sancho Panza. And at first he did live in Calcutta. But I've moved him in and out of a hundred different places. Which brings me back to the Bolivian Army standing on and around my little porch.

They accepted the imaginary friend thing. They were Bolivian. They had imagination too. The wolves held their peace. The lieutenant wanted to know where Desmond lived right now. I told him I couldn't remember. We've fallen out of touch lately. I thought I was telling the truth but I could hear the wolves start moaning.

"Mozambique?"

It was a wild guess. The lieutenant twisted his head aside to dodge the insult, lit a cigarette, took a deep hit. Then looked down the road and shook his head.

"Mozambique, huh."

"Honest to God," I said. "I don't remember sending him to Bolivia. What'd he do that got you after him? How did I get him out? I don't remember."

The wolves were restless. Starting to howl. The soldier out at the back of the pickup had his hand on the latch of the cage.

"Wait! Wait!" I said. "It's coming back! He's over in Moab! He's waiting tables at a place called the Sunset Grill!"

The lieutenant studied me hard. Looked for a long minute at the Burger King crown on my head. I could see it dawn on him that my wooden porch was starting to turn to quicksand. He waved his arm, turned down his thumb, and the soldier up on the road backed away from the howling coming from the bed of the truck.

"Sorry to disturb you," he said. "Have a nice day."

And they left. Were they headed for Moab? I had to get Desmond out of there before he ended up serving the Bolivian Army lunch. But where?

I called my agent.

"This guy Desmond really exists?" he asked.

"Yeah."

"And you can do anything you want with him?"

Will the Bolivian Army come back? Will I have Bolivian wolves come running up the dirt of the driveway when I answer the door in the morning? I don't know. Depends on Desmond.

"Pretty much," I told my agent.

"Make him a senior editor at Simon & Schuster. Random House. Knopf. Your choice. Do it now. I'll send him your stuff. We'll have a publisher tomorrow. What's his last name?"

"I don't know."

"Make one up."

ELVES IN THE RAFTERS, WHORES IN THE FIELDS

From where I stand in the kitchen there are cows
watching their long thoughts in the middle distance

of the slow blue afternoon. From where I stand in
my stockings there are power lines like black trails

left on the air by crows flying from the steel perch
of one tower to the next. From where I stand in my

own naked pool of daylight there are elves whoring
in the rafters and whores elving in the fields. See

here, I say, see here, my hand rising to the side of
my trembling face in shock at the feel of whiskers.

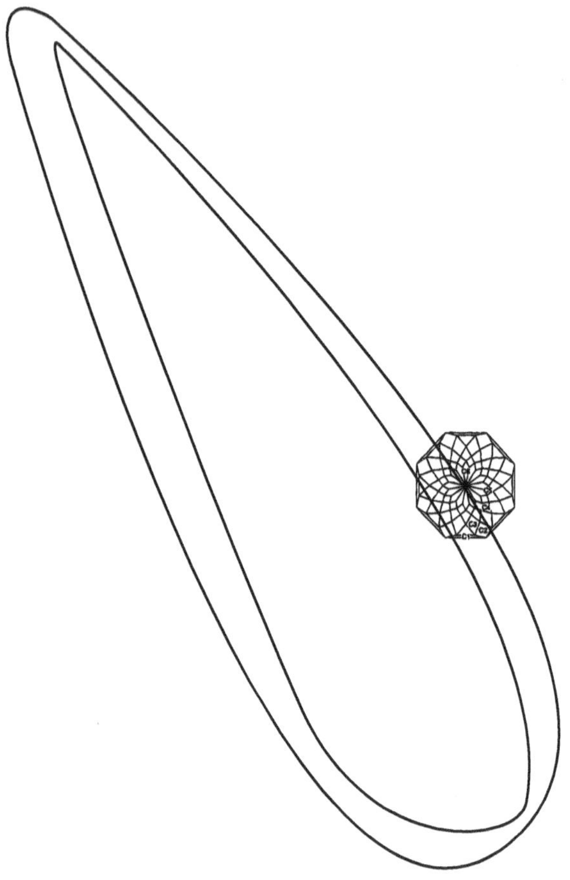

PEARLITA

For Billy

In your last few years in Salt Lake, before you blew up and walked away from everything your life had been, there were nights when your troubled history of conflict with the city would crowd in on you and leave you unable to sleep, your nerves crazed, barely able to breathe. To escape that suffocating claustrophobia of hate and rage and shame, you'd slip out of bed, quietly find your clothes in the dark, grab the two combination wrenches off the top of the fridge where you kept them, leave the apartment. You had an old race-prepped Porsche Speedster back then whose rusted frame and floor you'd reinforced with boilerplate, whose engine you'd rebuilt, whose suspension you'd lowered to where it had almost no travel, and whose wheels you'd widened to fit fat tires under it. You'd sand-blasted four coats of paint and underlying Bondo off its body and painted the bare metal with two rattle cans of red oxide primer.

In the dark garage behind the house you would take off the muffler and bolt the stinger—a straight open pipe that stuck out the back like the stinger on a bee—onto the manifold. You would idle it past the house and out the driveway to keep the deep eager crackle of the engine from waking your sleeping wife. You would ease the Porsche up through the empty streets of the city toward Emigration Canyon. Once there, you would open it up, full throat, this roaring mouth behind you that could never reach you, hearing the murmurs of anxious and curious animals as you passed the zoo and then raced up that twisting canyon to the crest of Little Mountain where you'd sometimes catch a glance of a couple standing next to a car in the moonlight before you were past them. Sometimes you'd name them. From there you'd race up and down canyon after canyon, the tires howling in the curves, for however long it took to clear yourself of everything, wash out all the bewildering chaos of hate and rage and shame.

Then and only then would you find your way to Parley's Canyon and come back down into the city on the four broad lanes of I-80, cleansed enough to pretend that you were coming from Cheyenne, Omaha, Chicago, some other city, pretending you'd never been to a city named Salt Lake, pretending you were only passing through on your way west into Nevada. All sense of history erased. It was how you would make the city livable again for a while.

Sometimes, heading down Parley's Canyon, you turned the radio on. Coasting mostly, your foot light on the pedal, the engine was quiet enough to let you hear the small speakers behind the seats. Sometimes you tuned it a show called the Nitecaps. It was a program you'd listened to before, an overnight talk show hosted by a soft spoken soothing guy named Herb Jepko, who took phone calls from people all across the country who worked graveyard shifts or were up like you for other reasons. They all called the moderator Herb. They talked about their aches and pains and illnesses and operations and misfortunes. They talked about how blessed they were to be alive. They asked about each other. Herb was a solicitous and sympathetic host—the father figure to a national family of lonely voices that come out of the dark from across America, voices looking for company and a place to belong this late at night.

That night, coming down Parley's from God knows what pretended city, you listened as a woman who sounded young call in. There was a shy and elegiac quality to her voice. The conversation went something like this.

"Hi, Herb. This is Pearlita."

"Well hello, Pearlita. Where are you calling from tonight?"

She named some rust belt city you can't remember. But she also mentioned a dashboard factory where she worked.

"Is this your first call to the Nitecaps?" Herb asked.

"Yes, Herb. The first time I got through."

"Well then, welcome to the Nitecaps, Pearlita. We're glad to hear from you."

"Thank you, Herb. I listen to your show every night."

"Thank you, Pearlita. By the way, that's a lovely name."

"Thank you, Herb. It means Little Pearl."

"Little Pearl. How very nice."

"Yeah. Except I'm not so little anymore."

"Well . . . "

In the silence of the dark you can hear people across the country listening intently.

"I put on some weight, Herb. I let myself go."

"It happens to the best of us."

"Yeah. I guess so. So my friends here at the dashboard factory, they call me Pearlotta now."

"Pearlotta?"

"Yeah. It means Lotta Pearl."

Pearlotta. The innocence in that name. You don't recall how the rest of the conversation went because you stopped listening. What you do remember was the feeling of an angel's hand on your head, whispering that you had nothing to fear, that everything would be all right, that everything would be forgiven. You just drove. And what else you remember is that somewhere along the way you started crying. You still don't know why. You know that it wasn't out of pity. You couldn't stop. You didn't want to. You cried the rest of the way down the canyon. The wind drove the tears back along your temples and dried them off your skin. You were still crying when the canyon walls abruptly fell away and opened up on the sudden immensity of the sea of light that was the only city you call home.

Billy, you thought, the name you gave the guy with the girl at the crest of Little Mountain. Billy, you thought, save us. Save us all.

IN HAVING LEARNED

In having learned, around the neighborhood
that seventeen and raped, I should not school
with their sweet teen, but with my father—could
he have changed my age and been less cruel?

I walk the backs of sidewalks, feel the blade
my father held against my cheek that hour—
how, like a dentist's white-frocked help, he said
my teeth would hold a child—his face was dour—

Rejoice. There is no learning quite like mine
in having caught my father's eye behind
this cervix—no, his blood was unlike wine
that left my cheek and down my thigh would find

This neighborhood, its plundered faces turned
away from having worked and having earned.

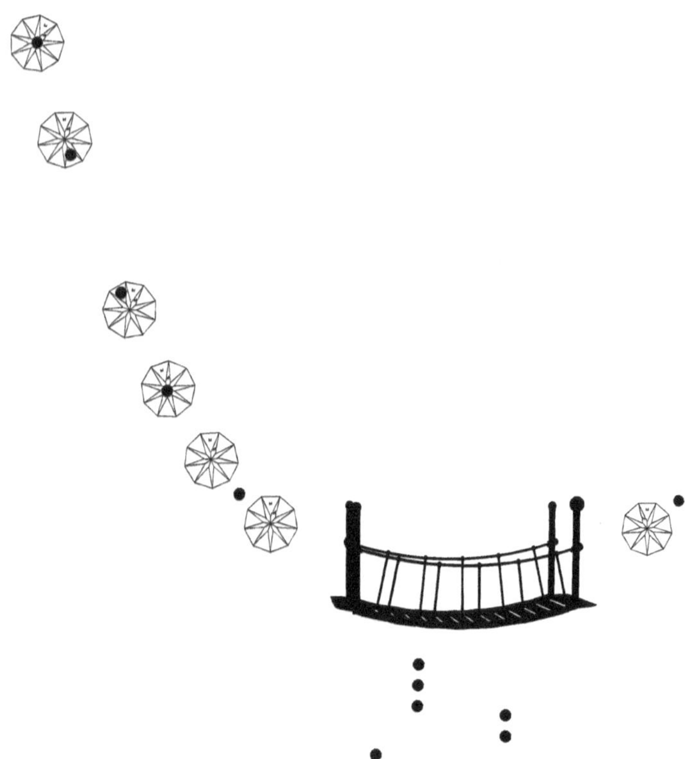

THE BRIDGE

Remember where you heard this: the night flies wide-eyed into its own surprising recognition of the squirrel, its cheeks ripe with seed, dead in the birdfeeder. The winged skunk describes a higher and wider circle each time it passes over the cloud-scarred face of the rising moon from where you stand, in the dark yard, a bag of Fritos half-eaten in your hand. The midnight truck defies the sound of its approach across the silver hand of the lake. In the porchlight stands a man in a used suit, the scalp riding scorched as a desert cliff above his ears, holding a briefcase of brochures for the sale of insurance, his finger trembling as it hovers like the conductor's baton over the opening strains of the Soviet National Anthem the illuminated doorbell is waiting to play. A train with its cargo of nostrils hurries like a poisoned rat along the edge of the Hudson. Overhead, a red Corolla follows an arched lane across the Tappan Zee, the floormat covered with the teeth of the driver, her hair white with pleasure, the gearshift whispering "dickhead dickhead" to the drumming of the expansion joints. A shotgun retires its stock against the soft inner shoulder of the man whose ears are safely out of reach in his wallet. The phone rings; the question you're asked is whether you think Republicans or Democrats are more prone to eat a nutritious breakfast. You say Africans; you hear the light glide of a wood burner along a woman's thin forearm; you realize that singing the alphabet sounds much like whistling through the mouth of your son's new skull at an auction for decent neighborhoods the man with the briefcase is waiting to rescue from behind their unlocked doors. A chair, a simple chair, one made of painted wood, steals into your bedroom from the kitchen; the question you're asked is what it means to you to walk to Chicago. Do you know? Does it conjure a bloodhound too old to tell us that the hanky at its nose was used to wipe its genitals? The black shock of hair crossing the Tappan Zee behind the Corolla's lowered eyes? The woman who knows that if she makes a U-turn on the bridge her car will turn to salt? The man who takes her money at the toll booth asks her for a ride. He sits beside her until he is dead, then gathers her teeth off the floor and has time to put them in her purse before he comes back to life at the border of Connecticut. You heard this from a man who plays rugby with a ball made of crushed aluminum.

BROWNIES

He made the mistake, once, of
telling her he liked her brownies.
That was the first batch. Telling
her, perhaps, of the hawk's habit
for circles, or of the first time
he'd danced, he'd eaten them hungry

for nothing else. The kitchen smelled
of topsoil. Because of the night's knock
against the hull of the house or
the carpenter's visit earlier
that day she increased the yield.
At three batches a day, he could
hear the rooster in the far corner
of the field he worked with the
small hoes of his teeth. When
she sowed them with hash
he would fill his pockets with rocks
and walk into the hills.

Coming home, his feet weary, he
wondered what he'd meant to say,
his shoes heel deep in
the arresting yield of topsoil,
the long laugh of the carpenter
falling toward him
from the highest room of the house.

THE CHINA DOLL

At the time this happened, there was one direct flight out of any airport around New York that would get you to Salt Lake City in time for you to have someone there—a high school buddy who'd gone into real estate, say, or an old music professor—buy lunch for you. That flight took off from Newark sometime after seven in the morning, and got you out to Salt Lake International at 11:45. From what I hear, the flight's been discontinued—Salt Lake's been in a kind of recession lately—but it was still on the roster the last time I saw my father.

My name is Frankie Loscher. I'm thirty-six years old and play trumpet in a jazz band. There are four of us, and we've played together about five years now, and our gigs are mostly out on the Island or in Jersey, but lately we've been getting more work in the city. I live with a woman named Jill in a second-floor studio on 30th Street off Third Avenue. We've been together for going on eleven years. Jill used to work on Wall Street. Now, though, she works at Tower Records, down on East 4th, and goes to a broadcasting school on West 26th three nights a week because she wants to be a disk jockey. The way she explains it is that she'd rather wear a headset than a suit, and play Eric Clapton rather than the market. You could say our neighborhood is funky—developers and Koreans have only lately begun gutting some of the rickety Irish joints and carting away the more dilapidated street-corner walkups—and you might say the same for the way we live. I own one suit. It was bought for me by my father, and I think I've worn it twice, once to a wedding, and the other time to my mother's funeral. Jill owns around seven or eight. Not one has had a reason to see daylight since the Tuesday she took her employee stock and left the highrise boneyard she used to ride the Number Six to every morning. On weeknights, when I'm not playing and she's not at school, we tend to hang out at this Irish bar called Buck's on Third Avenue. We used to drink at another Irish place, on 34th and Lex, a place called the Guardsman, but the building housing it came down just over a year ago.

The reason I mention all this, I guess, is that this seems to be the way you define yourself in New York: by what you do, where you live, who you hang out with. Where you're from, if you're from out of town, doesn't seem to count for much for long. After a year or two, you start saying you're from New York anyway, and it gets to where nobody really seems to have had a serious past before coming here, where nobody you know is really from anywhere else. People like David Letterman and Jane Pauley keep reminding us that they're from Indiana, but the reminders seem staged, and the place itself, used as a cachet, seems somehow falsified. For the rest of us, places like North Carolina, Arizona, and Texas seem quickly to lose their real geography, and become storybook places about which we tell a few increasingly fictionalized stories. It gets to where what matters is not so much where you're from, but how much of your life you've spent in New York.

The chance to see my father came up one night at a club down on Varick, below the Village, where the band was playing. A friend of Jill's in advertising was flying out to the coast to do a commercial for a new chain of outskirts Mexican restaurants. She wanted to know if I could fly out to Los Angeles and do this trumpet line they needed for the sound track. I thought it was a long way to go, and a lot of air fare to pay, for a single line of music. I remember thinking to myself the crazy world of advertising. While we were talking, though, I realized I could stop in Utah and see my father, and so I told her I'd be glad to do it.

My mother had died a little over two years ago. I hadn't been out to see my father, for one reason or another, since the funeral in Salt Lake, and the memory of his confusion and paralysis at the cemetery still fell uneasily, like some quick turn of wind along a pane of smashed glass, against this contradictory and obligatory backdrop of bleak faces and bright flowers that surround any fresh grave. Over the phone the next day he sounded thrilled when I told him I'd be stopping through around noon.

"Will I be free for lunch?" he said. "I'll make dead certain that I am, by golly."

By golly. It was an idiom, along with dead certain, that I'd heard him use almost all my life. He used the first to express responsibility, gravity, reliability, and he used the other to convey this circus air of an enormous and almost airborne enthusiasm, astonishment, or exasperation, as the tone of the moment required. Together, the two of them stood, like vocal signposts, at the opposite poles of his emotional range. He'd started using them soon after we'd first arrived in Utah, after his conversion to Mormonism in Switzerland, when he was learning simultaneously to be American and Mormon. By golly. Dead certain. He'd picked them up, but then he'd never left them behind the way other people pick up and move on to newer ways of putting an accent on things.

On the phone, I wanted to know if we could eat at the China Doll. The China Doll was a diner out on Redwood Road not far from where he worked. The two of us had met there for lunch occasionally while I was in school at the university up on the east side of Salt Lake. The China Doll was where, in this weekly rotation among its chartreuse and black naugahyde booths, my father and I had hashed out our own frequently brutal and always innocent version of the generational conflict that ended up being visited upon every father and son by the Sixties. Out in front of the place, off the edge of asphalt of Redwood Road, there stood this painted statue of what I guess they meant by a china doll. She stood probably thirty feet high and was made, much like the Statue of Liberty, out of sheet metal riveted to a frame. I remembered her ridiculously small waist and the way her black hair was bunned up to some absurd height above her sharp white face. And I remembered the way that her yellow and green and black kimono, sashed way too tight to pass for the way women wore them, gleamed in the early afternoon in the relentless sunlight you always get in Utah. The Doll was a place I'd come to see as a personal form of some religious shrine. It had seen its share of quiet and scathing violence pass back and forth between my father and me. But the Doll, perhaps for its neutrality, had also wielded some form of resolving power that I'd never experienced under the roof of any other building in the company of my father.

"The China Doll?" my father laughed. "Of course."

"You still eat lunch there?"

"Of course I still eat lunch there. In fact, I eat there more than ever. I was there a couple of days ago with Ron Bullins."

"So. It's a date."

"You can bet on it, Frankie."

I worked the night before the flight, put my trumpet away at somewhere after four that morning, caught a cab, and went straight through the Holland Tunnel out to Newark. It was raining but there wasn't any traffic. At the airport I bought a disposable razor and a toothbrush out of a vending machine. I shaved in the men's room and hoped that the smell of the smoke at the club would be out of my clothes by the time I got to Salt Lake. This old homeless guy, wearing one of those Beethoven sweatshirts nobody wears anymore, asked if he could use the razor, and started to tell me about his career as a founding editor at Road and Track Magazine. Then he cut himself, yelled, and went on to complain about what he seemed to have come to see as a world shortage of mirrors.

"You just can't find a goddamned mirror in a bathroom anymore these days," he said. "How in hell are you supposed to shave these days? Wait for a sunny day and use the hood of somebody's car? Use a goddamned bank window? Hell, you know what women are getting hit for these days? It's not their money. It's not their jewelry. It's for those goddamned little mirrors they carry around in their handbags. If they'd just leave them home, and word got around, you wouldn't see a crime rate in New York."

He may have been right. I'd noticed from different clubs I'd played that a lot of them didn't have mirrors in the men's room anymore. Maybe it had to do with the crime rate. Maybe owners were either tired of finding them busted or gone and having to replace them, or they just weren't putting them up in the first place. I didn't know. At the airport here it looked as though mirrors had never been in the blueprints. I'd shaved without one. But now I became aware of what I would look like in one. A Dire Straits teeshirt Jill had brought home from Tower. An old leather flight jacket. Generally, I took a sense of stupid but unavoidable pride in the fact that the jacket looked worn not because of this beating they give leather at the factory to make it look what they call stressed, but as a result of my long and real history with it. Now, in the white, shadowless light of the men's room, the creases and the bald spots made the jacket just look old and tawdry. My levis looked the same way. I opened my fly to make sure I was wearing underwear. I looked down to see what I was wearing for shoes. They were loafers and they looked passable. They even looked like I'd put some polish on them recently.

But there wasn't much point to the polish, because I turned out not to be wearing socks.

I don't know why the way I was dressed hadn't crossed my mind sooner. It could have been because my destination was a studio gig in L.A. and this was the way I'd dressed when I'd lived out there. It could have been because the chance to see my father had grown to enough of a preoccupation in itself to have pushed the formal incidentals out of my head. I thought of catching a cab back into town for a change of clothes. But it was already after five, rain was coming down hard, and with the rain, the morning traffic into Manhattan would already have started clogging the tunnels. I never would have made it back in time to Newark.

You get these times where you think of your life as a piecemeal kind of thing, as pieces of time laid out in a kind of line, the pieces defined by what you did with them. Sometimes they make sense together. Sometimes you can see some comprehensible pattern taking you from one piece to the next, some pattern that indicates, I guess, what passes for progress. At other times you simply have to take what you can from each of the pieces. The only thing worth taking from the two-hour piece I spent that morning waiting for my flight was the news that they don't sell socks between five and seven A.M. at Newark International. At least not on a Friday. Coffee, though, was another story. I had to be alert to meet my father, and by the time I got on the plane, four cups of machine grade caffeine were looking for my nervous system.

On the flight, I tried not to fall asleep before the coffee took hold. Anything less than seven hours of sleep, especially in the daytime, has always seemed too much like a nap to me, and I've never come out of a nap without having to take what's left of the day to work off the stupor. Arrival time, and my father, were only around five hours away. I got a shoeshine rag from the stewardess and polished my trumpet. There was the outside possibility that my father would ask to see it. At least it would show on my trumpet that I'd made some gesture of recognition toward the importance of the visit.

But then much of how I'd spend the flight would be in exactly that kind of gesture. I already knew I'd have to be alert. Now, I suppose, it was time to do some homework. Now, away from New York and its unavoidable and sad potential for distorting what the rest of the country was like, it was time to sit back, get used to the sound of the low gale from the engines, watch a country one state after another first come awake and then go to work this morning at the end of March, and do some homework. Forces as unforgiving and real as a bomb's had gradually exploded our family out across the United States more than ten years ago. The memory of their power, much like some repulsive electrical field, still held all five of my father's children out away from any serious longing to live in Salt Lake again. I had to get to know them again.

Unlike me, my mother had been an inveterate napper. At three o'clock every afternoon, she would give the house a quick tour to make certain that things were in relative order, then excuse herself for the hour and disappear into the bedroom. That afternoon hour, for which the house was to remain inviolably still, was left ingrained enough that it took me years after moving away to outgrow the sense of an urgent and mandated hush when the afternoon would touch upon that hour. At the end of the hour, around four, we would know that she was up again, fresh, restored, when we would hear, from wherever we were in the house or in the yard, the galvanizing and unmistakably arresting authority of her hands on the keys of her piano, playing the strict and limpid opening of some sonata or intermezzo only as someone schooled in Europe would play them.

She had taught piano in Switzerland. There, in the music room we had, hung on the wall above her large black Boesendorfer grand, a savage, brooding and enormous tapestry, depicting a boar hunt in the Black Forest, had rested its murderous prospect on the awkward and resistant shyness of children trying to make habitual to their fingers the odd configurations of Hanon's scales and arpeggios and chords. I had been one of them. When we left Switzerland, after my father was converted to the Mormon faith and chose to pursue the Kingdom of Heaven in Utah, the piano came with us. She wanted to teach there. The tapestry, along with any interest I had tried to conjure for the keyboard, stayed behind. I was four years old.

In Utah, in the first small house, the Boesendorfer had to be put in the unfinished basement; there was no room for it upstairs. My mother got a dehumidifier for Christmas that first year to keep the different woods from being damaged by the dampness. Headstrong and indifferent to public opinion, it didn't occur to her that it might do lasting social damage to her children to have to live in the only house in the neighborhood with a piano instead of a ping-pong table in the basement. Nor did she understand that the only concert hall in which we might ever be able to perform would have to be built of studs of raw lumber, exposed aluminum heating ducts and electrical wiring, and plywood-grained concrete walls. Seated next to her, practicing selections from this book called Czerny's School of Velocity those first few months in Utah before she took my lack of interest to be as serious and irreversible a handicap as being born without fingers, I would wonder how to explain this to the dark-haired woman watching my hands, the woman headstrong enough to have refused to leave Switzerland without her piano.

She eventually succeeded at raising exactly the children she wanted; whatever instruments we played would fall to us easily as a result of my mother's scrupulous and vigorous enthusiasm for the adventure of music. What she could not succeed at passing along to us, though, was a stubborn conviction that the piano was the only instrument truly suited to the scope of this adventure. To her the piano was sovereign. It was the instrument for which the best of the world's good music had been written. We all started out, for lack of any countermanding evidence, by agreeing with her. But we all ended up recanting. My sisters both learned cello in high school and still involve themselves in the music societies of the towns out in California where they now live. I have a brother in Houston who plays jazz flute. The last of her five children, my other brother, took up guitar and headed for Chicago, where he enrolled in music school.

Growing up in a house that seemed capable of withstanding any dire act of God or nature merely because of the physical ballast a concert grand in the basement seems to give to a house, I think we came, simply, to be interested in less imposing and more portable instruments. There was, of course, no plausible or legitimate way to argue for the portability of a trumpet or a cello to a woman who had brought a grand piano all the way across the Atlantic, the Great Plains, and the Rocky Mountains. There were, however, under the Constitution of the United States as we understood it, things you had the inalienable right as a child to refuse to inherit. And that was where we finally made our stand against the Boesendorfer. Each of us had this portent, I guess, of some explosion a few years down the road; each of us looked for the ability to travel light, and not without music, when the time for the explosion came.

A parent's belief can pose its own entirely genuine danger when that belief is transfigured with any real or obvious force into what parents hope for in their children. Both my parents, for lack of a better word, were guilty of this. My mother wielded her belief in the Boesendorfer almost until she died. She took great satisfaction in discovering imaginative ways to let us know we'd picked up inferior instruments. My sisters would practice cello at home and my mother would take some heavy skillet out to the back yard and thrash the bushes pretending there were mutant wolves to drive away. A little improvised line from my brother's flute would start her off on a form of improvisation of her own about modern-day troubadours. Jazz musicians were merchants of musical chaos. Drugs hadn't crossed her horizon yet, but alcoholism and venereal disease, she would say when her form was at its peak, would mark the rites of passage of my brother's life. To give some credit to her insights, it should be said, I suppose, that he did have some trouble. But he was able to turn a degree in computer science and an instinct for business into a data processing service that made him rich enough by the time he was twenty-five to send my parents back to Europe for the summer.

Then there was me. My trumpet, she said, would put her in her grave. My trumpet would be the instrument of her death. I imagine her allusions were to Joshua or to Gabriel or to the long fanfare of awful brass that to decades of Christians was the sign that the lions were hungry. Luckily, we were left to believe that at least some of this was good-natured. Luckily, she was a good loser, and before the actual event of her death she got to where she was able to concede and even endorse our musical independence.

The danger posed by my father resided in his relentless and driving belief in the sovereign truth of Mormon doctrine. Like my mother, he had also had to watch the five of us respond to something different, something more our own. Unlike my mother, who took to her grave a truce with the musical waywardness of her children, my father would never be able to regard our departure from his faith with any lightness. He had come to the States responding to a new and shiny doctrine that had promised him the possibility of a life after death far more radiant and lovely than what he'd been led to expect of the bleak and strictured Calvinist heavens of Switzerland. That doctrine had not only refreshed for him the possibility of his own immortality—he'd grown up believing in that already— but had introduced to him the possibility of immortal unity for his family. The bonds of his family, the doctrine promised, could be made immune against death. The potency of his fatherhood was as infinite as his soul. We would not revert, in the afterlife, to adoring and devoted children of God, but would remain his.

That promise meant everything. On its wings, he abandoned his professorship in history at the University of Zurich, and learned, in Utah, out of his incompetence in English and the necessity for providing for us immediately, the first reasonable trade that came his way. What that trade turned out to be could not have mattered less to him. He had just been handed an opportunity so enduring—that of immortal fatherhood—that it could not have mattered less what it was that would occupy the comparatively trivial and brief interval between his arrival in Utah and his retirement. The trade turned out to be bookkeeping. He could keep up with history on the side. What mattered was that his family, rather than something he had simply borrowed from God, was something he now owned. Nothing could have made more sense. Nothing could have been more natural.

There were rules, of course. There were conditions which each of us would have to meet. Over the ensuing years, as my father saw his children fail with increasing resolve to live up to them, they became conditions that had seemed simple enough at the outset but in the end would leave heavy and restless lines in a face that had come from Europe boyish. Mormon doctrine enumerated them in a list as practical and logical as the instructions you follow to hook up a VCR or cook a meat loaf. Baptism at the age of eight. Ordination of the sons into the Mormon Priesthood. Marriage, for both the sons and daughters, in the Temple. Full tithing. A life for every member of the family of exemplary abstinence from smoking and drinking and adultery and, above all, from religious doubt. From looking at the Church publications my father still mails out to each of us in a monthly package, the signs are hard to avoid that since the Second World War some letup in the required strictness of observance of some of the more minor conditions has steadily been taking place. But that letup seems to have overlooked, in its subtle and gradual way, the fact that the chastened and closely guarded atmosphere of postwar Europe was the atmosphere in which my father's faith was cast.

In Salt Lake, after the first small house, the houses he went on to buy continued to be modest. And while they would never have the room upstairs to house the Boesendorfer, the last of them, at least, had a finished basement. He went on being deferential to his American neighbors. Sadly, this deference seemed scarred by a deep humility which at times would take a heartbreakingly servile turn, but my father was trying to raise his family by rules that would ensure our immortal togetherness. If his deference was ever a source of embarrassment to his family, it never seemed to bother him. Modesty—a reluctance to reveal worldly ambitions—was one of those rules. He always kept the paths that led to the doors of our houses lined with rosebushes. He sent us to local public schools. He bought Chevrolets and used them to drive us to Disneyland, to Yellowstone, to Hoover Dam. He loved being an American. He loved the United States and carried out his duties as one of its modest citizens in all the detail work expected of that role.

But he had come to it as a convert, as a traveler, as someone in pursuit of the Kingdom of Heaven, and there were times where he seemed to regard Utah itself as a sort of railroad station on the border of a foreign country at which his papers had to undergo the long and rigorous scrutiny of suspicious officials. At times like those, like any father with a travel itinerary and small children in tow, his greatest concern was not to let us wander too far out of sight. Where he deferred to his neighbors with a great deal of jocularity, he was stern, intense, and watchful at the dinner table. He'd come from a country which, although neutral, had seen bombs fall on its railroad stations. He was now on the path toward the greatest promise life could possibly offer his family. When he listened to the Church authorities talk gravely of the pitfalls along the way, I could tell, from seeing the haunted and vigilant thoughtfulness in his broad face, that he was fleshing out this abstract spiritual path with the quite real craters and rubble of the war.

This was where my father applied that resource of new industriousness every expatriate discovers in coming to America. Not to the pursuit, like others, of unprecedented earthly riches, but to the tireless and immaculate fulfillment of what Mormon doctrine promised if he could adroitly steer his family through the hazards of the times. My brothers and I, beginning at the age of twelve and then on three more occasions over the next seven years, were put through the ranks of the Priesthood. I remember sitting on a folding chair in one of the classrooms at the chapel with the hands of six or seven of my father's fellow Priesthood bearers stacked on my head. I remember looking at their shoes, at their pockets, at their belts, watching their shirts collapse and expand as they breathed and hearing, with its European accent, its poorly disguised pride, and its recognition that the task at hand required consummate humility, my father's voice. "We, the Elders of Israel," he would begin, "in the name of Jesus Christ, and by the power of the Holy Melchizedek Priesthood vested in us, hereby lay our hands upon your head and confer upon you . . . " Later, as we each reached nineteen, my brothers and I were returned to Europe, as missionaries, to spend a stretch of two years knocking on doors in cities like Vienna, Berlin, and Basel. His daughters were told, when they were ready to go to college, that the only institution where they could expect my father's help with expenses was Brigham Young University. Each of us tried to strike a compromise. By the time I reached my early twenties, the family had exploded, and all of us were gone.

The Church News. The Improvement Era. The Ensign. As each of us looked for separate futures, these were some of the publications that would track us from state to state, from city to city, from address to address over the years, together with clippings from out-of-state newspapers which attested to the quality of life in Utah, the friendliness and cleanliness of the people, the low rate of cancer in the state, the business and architectural boom that was gathering head in Salt Lake, the cultural advances being made beneath the great dome of the Tabernacle. There was one clipping about breaking ground for the Salt Lake Sheraton. Another clipping celebrated the promotion of the Salt Lake airport to international status.

My father had lost us. That his loss could be written off as nothing more than the religious disaffiliation of his children—a common thing in America—didn't mean that the depth of his sense of failure, his abjectness, was any more shallow than what it is for the father whose son brodies off the Brooklyn Bridge or whose daughter is found dead in a Times Square stairwell. His doctrine placed uncompromisingly high stakes on a break with the faith. At nineteen, cloistered inside the Salt Lake mission home with maybe two hundred other brand new missionaries, I listened to advice on how to take care of my feet, what kind of shoes to buy, what suit material best withstood the wear and tear imposed by the seat of a bicycle, and any number of lectures on the gravity of faith. One anecdote, used a number of times to drive this gravity home, told about some mother whose parting declaration to her son as he boarded his flight out of Utah for some foreign destination was that she would rather see him come home in a coffin than return in any way dishonored. This, as the Church saw it, was motherly love at its loveliest and strongest. My father had lost us. Given the ardor of his faith in a church that could look at death more readily than it could at weakness, he was helpless to see it any other way.

But he was a man whose vision had brought his family from the other side of the world to a remote enclave of the Rockies. He was a man whose greatest asset all along had been hope. I knew from my youth that his persuasive powers were capable of working with whatever raw material was at hand. At Disneyland he'd pointed out to me the suggestion of a house of worship in the spires of Tinkerbell's Castle. The loss of his children now had merely made necessary the expansion and refinement of those powers. We had hurt him deeply. But we had also thrown him back on an inestimable reserve of hope. Now I was visiting him. I was passing through. I could be thinking possibly of coming back. On the flight that morning, thinking over my father's helpless predilection for the five of us, I understood that this was behind my wanting to be alert when I met him. After we landed, I saw him there, waiting for me, at the end of a velvet rope that marked the gate.

There is no authentic way to describe what I felt go through me when we first embraced. Conscious, still, of people around us that I'd spent the last few hours with, I made some clumsy joke which he didn't even try to answer. After that, embracing him was more compelling than anything I could remember having touched in New York for a long time. I thought involuntarily about moving back to Salt Lake. Hugging my father struck me as something I should have the right to exercise daily. My nose was up against his hair and collar. I smelled the river of scents in which I'd experienced the buoyancy and current of my childhood. Aftershave, hair tonic, the bitter smell of the air-conditioned office, these were tributaries to that river, but its strongest current was his sour and ambrosial odor as a male, an odor whose restless urgencies no amount of store-bought scents could have completely concealed. When we let go of one another, I realized that my own hair probably still stank of tobacco. I also realized that I hadn't set my trumpet case down, and that I'd struck him across the back with it.

"I hope I didn't hurt you with this," I said.

"No, Frankie," he said, smiling broadly and looking me in the face. "You could never hurt me. I don't have to tell you that."

"It's been a long time."

"It certainly has, by golly," he said. "How's Jill? Home seeing to the bills while you're out running around the country?"

"She's fine, Dad. She says hello. She's going to broadcasting school."

"I know. She wrote me about it."

He was shorter than what I remembered or expected, and his hair, wavy still, trimmed, combed back as always off his forehead, was more completely gray. His face had also changed. Although in its ample breadth there would always be the open and guileless bonework of a boy beneath the unmistakable facial skin of someone who's been a father for almost forty years, it was more vigorously lined than I wanted to admit. In the last few years it had started to become apparent to me that this would be my face as well. Now, though, more than I ever had, I saw the particularity of his face. No other man on earth could have lived my father's specific life. He had lost that dimension for me that made fathers universal and alike. Maybe the fact that he was a widower now, that he lived by himself again, made this easier to see. Over my long periods away from him, or at times when I wondered what it might have been like to grow up Catholic or Baptist, I had occasionally put other men in his place. I saw now that this had been out of convenience. He and I were stuck with one another.

"You had a good flight? Did you get any sleep? They gave you something to eat?" With an awkward jocularity he started to laugh, and he slapped me lightly on the shoulder to underscore the fact that what was coming was a joke. "Or did they take one look at you and think that this bum doesn't deserve breakfast?"

"They served me breakfast," I said, my own laugh involuntary. "They didn't tell me what they thought of me."

He was still laughing. "Well," he said, and made a deliberate point of looking me up and down, "it certainly looks as if they've finally deregulated the airlines, by golly."

He'd lost weight. He'd lost a good deal of weight. It struck me as a loss that my mother, one of whose more bitter and lasting crusades had been to get him into exactly this condition, hadn't lived to see him this fit and trim and healthy. He was dressed to within the width of a hair to walking off the page of a magazine for men's fashions. He was wearing a pink suit, but he'd chosen a shirt and tie to go with it that made the color look conservative rather than foppish. His tasseled loafers were the kind of shoes where you laid down a lot of money merely for the simplicity of the style. The polish on them was high enough to make them appear that they'd been lacquered.

"From the way you look," I said, "they haven't deregulated a thing at the office. Not by a long shot. You look great."

"Thank you. Coming from a New Yorker, Frankie, that is a real compliment. What is Dire Straits?" We'd stepped back away from one another, and he was looking at my teeshirt.

"It's a rock group. When did you start wearing pink?"

"Why, when they started to wear it in New York," he said. "A couple of months ago? You haven't noticed? Come. Let's go get your luggage. We don't have enough time as it is. Let's go. Let me have your ticket."

"Yeah. I didn't bring any luggage. But let me get my bearings for a minute."

"You can get your bearings in the car. Let's go. I've got to get back to the office soon, by golly."

Something was changing, changing rapidly, rapidly enough that I felt my stomach knot the way it does when I first discover I've just lost something or had something stolen. There was more to it than the brusqueness with which he'd just insisted on leaving. It was more as though the announcement of some personal calamity had come over the public address system in some language that, of the two of us, only he understood. Some maneuvering of recrimination and doubt had started to run through his features. Certain lines in his forehead and around his mouth had suddenly risen from their placid and smiling smoothness into a vivid crossfire of relief. It hadn't occurred to me yet that we'd met and remained right in the path of passengers still getting off the flight. Carry-on luggage was being banged against the backs of my legs. There were reunions other than ours going on around us. When I saw him divert a poorly concealed and terribly flustered glance in the same direction more than once, and turned to look, I knew what was the matter.

They are almost impossible to miss once you've been one. I've never been able to put a finger on what sets them apart from other Americans in suits. They would tell you it was their testimony of the truth of Mormon doctrine. But the truth might be, simply, that other Americans who wear suits on a daily basis generally tend to be older than nineteen or twenty. It's also almost impossible to take a direct flight from New York to Salt Lake without one or two or more of them being on board, returning from one of the mission fields of Europe. I'd forgotten about this. The one who'd made the flight with me, I saw now, was blond, good-looking, had on a gray European suit, and was carrying a Book of Mormon. I wondered if he had tried to convert somebody on the plane. I recalled being told that we shouldn't miss even this transient an opportunity to look for a convert. He was surrounded and almost engulfed by a crowd of loving and boisterous relatives, maybe forty feet away from where my father and I were standing.

A girl, maybe twenty years old, radiant and beautiful, stood back away from the crowd, apparently waiting her turn. Grabbed by this old and savage instinct I didn't realize was still there and consequently couldn't have avoided, I understood that waiting was her strength, that waiting was an aura she'd carried with all the noble and somber spectacle usually reserved for a pregnant woman, that what had construed her two-year contribution to the success of her boyfriend's mission had been the effort and deprivation of waiting. Waiting. It was what gave her the radiance, false as tin, on which she now seemed poised.

I thought of my sister Janie. When we were kids my father had managed to find, from among the herds of kids in the neighborhood, an example for each of us to emulate. Janie had grown up pitted by my father against the example of this girl. Janie, as it is with any example, had grown up always falling short of hers. At Brigham Young University, naive to the slick and lurid hypocrites you find at any religious school, she was gang raped one night a month into her freshman year by her roommate's boyfriend and his buddies. Her roommate, using, I imagine, familiar religious tools, took care of the possibility that Janie might go to the police by explaining to her that the rape was her fault, and that the penalty for bringing rape down on yourself was expulsion from Brigham Young. Janie fled the next day to New York. For the first two months she was there, we didn't know where she was. Then she wrote. She was waitressing and doing volunteer work at something called a Phoenix House. She was working with addicts. She had something to do with keeping a mentally handicapped teenage girl from being sold around as a prostitute by the mob. What she said about Brigham Young was that she simply hadn't fit in. Shame over having wasted the money my father had spent on tuition and housing had kept her from coming home. The same shame, along with wanting to protect her family from the worry and grief attendant with knowing that she was living on the street, had kept her from writing earlier. She'd just found a place to live with an older woman who was very nice to her. In a sentence to my mother, she wrote that she'd taken her cello along, and that she'd found a safe place to store it for the two months she'd been homeless.

I remember thinking, reading her first letter, that our real interest then had been in knowing whether she was alive at all. I also knew that another reason she hadn't written until she had an address was to protect herself from being compared again to Paula Swenson, the girl my father had picked as Janie's example, a girl Janie would otherwise have been able to call a friend, until her life was stable enough to withstand the devastating news that she hadn't measured up again. Janie stayed in New York, determined to measure up on the only terms available to her, those she happened to have been born to, for five years. She waitressed two or three jobs at a time, eventually got her own apartment, earned a degree at Hunter in social work, and did volunteer work when she had the time. One night, following an afternoon on which she'd found one of her cases dead in a Lower East Side hallway, she came home to her own apartment. Two young guys crashed the front door before she had a chance to latch it and forced her at knifepoint to take them to her apartment. They turned the apartment over. One of them held her while the other one cut her cat's throat. They asked where her money was. She didn't have any, she kept insisting, and so they beat her, badly enough to finally make her think that her home held out more sanctuary than New York. I was living in Salt Lake then, busy with being half of a happily but briefly married Mormon couple, and Janie called from someplace called La Guardia. I drove out to the airport alone to meet her flight. She was carrying her cello. Apparently, the guys who had hurt her had sensed some unforgiving family power in the instrument, because they had left it alone. It had been a week since she'd been beaten. But her face had been beaten so bad I could still barely look at her. She walked with a limp. The limp and the damage to her face would heal. But that wasn't the difference in Janie that struck me the hardest that night. It was this hard and shameless and controlled wildness in her brown eyes. The Sixties, I realize now, had just come home to the Loschers.

For anything my family might lack by way of just leaving each other alone, letting each other live, and knowing how to be subtle about suggesting what we find wrong with each other, the one time we really pull together and perform is when one of us is down and out. I call it circling the wagons. It's beautiful to watch. It's even better to participate. I came home from my mission in Austria having left my virginity in a room of a hotel in Vienna called the Rabe. I still had six months to go before my two years were up. I don't remember trying to convert anyone on the flight home, but I remember the stares I got the first time I showed up at church, from neighbors who carried missionary calendars in their heads. It was the first time I'd ever heard my mother tell someone to go to hell. My father ran interference for me when the authorities tried to tell me that a required step in my rehabilitation was to stand at the pulpit before the congregation, tell the story behind the fact that I was home early, and ask for their forgiveness. "These brothers and sisters, your neighbors, supported your son," he was told. "They have the right to know what happened." "They supported my son?" my father shot back. "Let me see their receipts. Show me their cancelled checks. In fact, show me one letter he received from one of my neighbors. Yes,

Sister Hohmann sent him a couple of packages, and if you really believe she needs to have him tell her why he was excommunicated, I'll see that he tells her. But nobody else. He's not a curiosity."

This same spirit, purposeful, fierce, its raw expression not crippled by humility, prevailed for Janie. My parents took her in, and for the time it took for her to heal and get back on her feet, we circled the wagons against the whooping cries of the neighbors, against the bright clay paint they'd smeared on their faces. "Hello, Theresa," a neighbor woman said to my mother, having used the telephone to penetrate the guarded house. "I heard about Janie and wanted you to know how bad I felt for you. There's a rumor going around that she's pregnant with a black man's child. I just wanted you to know that if it's not true I'll do my best to dispel it." "I wouldn't want to make a liar out of you," my mother said. Then she hung up the phone on a friend she wouldn't speak to again in her life.

An example was never brought up to Janie during her recovery. When the wagons were circled, there wasn't a kid around who was up to snuff with the Loscher kids. It was that simple. Not long after Janie found a job and a place of her own again, however, my father and I met for lunch and had a brief and scathing argument, and I saw how quickly victories like this were over, how suddenly they were forgotten, how abruptly my family's instinct for aggression, survival, and triumph could be wrapped away again in oilcloth. It was time to get the wagons moving again, I guess, time to get on with the journey. The argument took place at the China Doll on a dreary afternoon in winter. In the booth behind me, a woman with platinum hair, thighs that rose like dolphins out of her short skirt, and a voice full of brass was talking about Disneyland to an emaciated-looking guy in a cowboy hat.

"All I know," my father said, "is that if Janie had stayed at Brigham Young, this would not have happened. I don't understand it. Paula Swenson stayed there, met a young man and waited for him to return from his mission, married him in the Temple, and is having another baby."

"Yes," I said. "And she'll end up like everyone else you look up to. Never having made much difference." It felt disgusting and demeaning to attack Paula, a girl whose brother had been my friend for years, but Janie had to be defended. "Except to bring another tithe payer into the Church."

"So," my father retorted. "Janie made a difference. She runs off to New York, gets herself beat up, and then comes running back home. Now that's what I call making a difference. I think there's some work you need to do on what it means to make a difference. I think you're on your high horse again."

Either I hadn't known yet what was done to Janie at his cherished Brigham Young or I'd promised her by then to never tell the parents.

"You son of a bitch," I said. It was the first time I'd sworn at my father. Talk of Disneyland behind me came quickly to a halt. "She spent five years there, on her own, in this demonstration of guts and self-reliance the likes of which Paula Swenson won't see in a hundred years. You know what her last job there was? You know she was working to stop this mental hospital there from using its less retarded girls as prostitutes? Yes. Janie wrote you that. But since it doesn't have the sanction of your god damned church, it was a lot of meaningless crap. It was worse than that. It was some perversion of the faith. It was a sin or something. Come on, Dad. Tell me what you think it was. Let me hear your expert opinion on Christianity." I knew I had the attention of several neighboring booths. I'd managed to keep my voice low, and more or less level, but there's a list of buzzwords out there that will cut straight through the noisiest air of any diner on the Salt Lake outskirts. Church was one of them. "You son of a bitch," I repeated. I stood up, stared back at the woman behind me until she looked back at her outskirts cowboy, and picked up the flimsy green receipt. "Let's get out of here. We can finish this in the car."

I drove him back to his office. There was nothing to finish. I stopped the car in front of the glass door of the Deseret Press build-ing, an extended, low-profile affair where the publications for the Church were ground out. He pulled himself out of the car and shut the door and leaned back in through the open window. "Well, I learned something today," he said, raising his voice to be heard above a departing truck. "I learned the way a returned missionary speaks to his father. He calls him a son of a bitch, by golly."

At the airport, I watched now as my father grappled with the reunion going on across the floor from us, with the presence of a returning missionary, his family, and his imminent bride, strangers who all my life had drawn from him easily the unconditional and unreserved admiration Janie and the rest of us had always wanted and worked for. He needed to leave. I knew that. There with this one example of his own family, me, he didn't want to be observed.

I needed to get out of there too. In the face, once again, of his admiration of strangers, I felt a savage and crawling hatred of them, a familiar hatred I thought I'd outgrown. It seemed like I'd flown out from Newark naively, directly into the teeth of some truth about myself, and that I'd just placed my father between its jaws. The returning missionary and his girlfriend and family had done nothing ostensible to cause my father his embarrassment or to warrant his helpless adulation. They deserved my hatred even less. There were better things to do. I'd flown home from my own mission excommu-nicated and I'd gone through the strict probationary period required to become a Mormon again. Then, a year or two later, I'd walked away on my own. Nothing short of walking back again would make this up to my father. And nothing could have been less likely or even possible for me. But there were opportunities for smaller gestures.

"Excuse me for a minute, Dad," I said.

I set my trumpet case down near my father's shoes and crossed the polished stretch of the airport floor toward the reunion. The girl stared at me. "Excuse me," I said, and relatives began giving way, melting back as I touched their shoulders. For a moment, for the way they moved away, I could have been on the Number 6, moving toward the door to get off at Park and 28th. I might have wished I was. Then I reached the missionary. I'd startled him. I knew that. It was only natural that my intrusion would. But two years' worth of practice at the smiling imperturbability I'd learned on my own mission kept his expression from showing this.

"Congratulations. I noticed you on the plane, but I failed to take the chance to congratulate you then. Welcome home."

"Thank you," he said, grinning, pumping my hand. "Thanks very much. It's real good to be back in Zion again."

"I know. I've been away a while myself. Where did you happen to serve?"

"France," he said. "My name's Elder Hall. Actually, its James Hall. Jim. Guess I've got to start getting used to that again."

"I'm Frankie Loscher. That's my dad over there, standing next to the little suitcase. I guess I'm speaking for both of us by saying congratulations."

"These are my folks. Brother and Sister Hall. Hey, why don't you get your dad over here to say hello?"

The party of Jim Hall's relatives opened back, on cue, in the direction of my father. I watched as he rallied together a facial expression I had forgotten how indelibly well I knew. He picked up my trumpet case and crossed the floor between us. The girl watched him also. Waiting seemed, finally, to have put her in some kind of peril. Restless, she was shifting her weight from one white shoe to the other, starting to look a little elusive, starting to look around.

"These are the Halls," I said, to my father. "This is Jim. He just got back from France. These are his parents." I turned to the Halls. "This is my father," I said. "Harold Loscher."

Once again, as though everything that had taken place in the spread of the maybe fifteen years that stood between our argument about

Janie and this bright Friday afternoon in Utah had simply fallen through some crack we hadn't known was there, my father and I were riding along in silence. He was driving the blue Volkswagen Rabbit he'd written about having purchased. The webbed nylon bandolier of the shoulder strap, which had jumped out at me when I'd opened the door, was slung diagonally across my chest. My father had climbed in behind the wheel and adjusted his seat back and forth. I first wondered why, since he was the only driver, and when it struck me that this was what he'd had to do when everybody in the family was driving his car, I felt like I wanted him in my arms again. Mozart was on the cassette deck as we left the airport along the winding access road and then merged in with the faster traffic on the old concrete highway that went in toward the city. My eyes were having trouble getting used to the hard brilliance of the Utah sun.

"Well, it was nice of the Halls to ask us to come have lunch with them," I finally said, "I don't think they really intended it to happen, but it was nice of them to ask."

"Yes," he said. "They were very thoughtful."

"They were interested in hearing about Switzerland."

"Yes."

I looked over at him. Much of the confidence we'd had between us the first few moments at the airport had left his face. Doubt, now, and his particular brand of guilt—guilt for whatever it was that people like the Halls could put him in doubt of—had begun to play skittishly across his face, a face which still retained this open breadth, which still was flushed with this irrepressible joy at my being here, but which could no longer count serenity among its illuminating attributes.

"What have you been up to?" I asked. "Besides work?"

"Oh, this and that," he said, careful not to take too much of his attention away from his driving. I just sat waiting. Familiar places were going by outside the windshield. The long low building whose chestnut-colored bricks housed Litton Industries. The KOA campground that catered to families who had come across the desert from Nevada. The Pilot Cafe. Its dilapidated World War II fighter plane was still on the platform out in front. The Norwood Lounge. Before going out to Chicago, my brother Stevie had played guitar there with a country western band for a year. Seeing the place now, in the sunlight in the middle of the day, closed and bleak, its cinderblock walls sprawled out to the size of a bowling alley, I wondered how much point there had been to the harsh and grueling family violence that Stevie's working in a nightclub initially had given rise to. Then we were turning onto Redwood Road, turning and heading south along the outskirts toward the China Doll.

"I spoke at another funeral yesterday," my father said.

"Whose?"

"Do you remember Brother Steenblick? He was the bishop of the Seventh Ward when we first came to Utah. Well, you might have been too young to remember him, but the poor man died last week after a long struggle with Parkinson's disease. Yesterday he was buried."

"And you were asked to speak?"

"That's right. Don't ask me why. He was well known and he was very highly regarded in the Church. I'm certain that his widow had her pick of several authorities. Perhaps even one of the apostles. But for some reason she asked me. One of the least deserving and accomplished friends her husband had. I tried to tell her this but she wouldn't listen. I tell you, Frankie, I worked night and day on that speech. I'm not an authority by any means. And so I had to think of those people out in the audience who would see me at the pulpit and wonder what business it was of mine to speak on behalf of their feelings for Brother Steenblick."

"You were asked to. That's all they needed to know."

My father smiled at the windshield. With his face in profile I still saw how much patience he'd just had to harness.

"No, Frankie, that is not all they needed to know," he said. "I was there as a stranger to most of them. An outsider. But my preparation must have paid off, because after the service, several of them made the point of coming forward to tell me how my speech had touched them. In fact, no less an authority than Fred Leatham came up to me to shake my hand, and said that he couldn't remember when he'd heard a better tribute at a funeral. I hadn't even known he was there. Just imagine that, Frankie. A man of his position and with his schedule, taking the time to attend the funeral of an old friend. Not only that, but then not thinking twice about shaking the hand of a complete stranger. A man who speaks to hundreds of thousands of people at a time at General Conference, and here he is, telling an old foreigner what a good speaker he is. By golly, Frankie, it was one of the thrills of a lifetime yesterday. I put a copy of the speech in the mail to you this morning. You'll have to forgive me for bragging."

He was smiling again. This time he was smiling to himself and slowly turning his head back and forth in disbelief, as if what he had happen to him yesterday had truly been phenomenal and unique, as strange and wonderful and undeserved a blessing as the miraculous bestowal of sight on a man who all his life had believed that his blindness was connected with original sin. It wasn't true that he was a stranger to the authorities or in the circles of the sick and dying. It wasn't true that an authority such as Leatham was a more practiced or accomplished public speaker. I knew this. I knew this because my father sent me copies of Leatham's speeches in the mail. My father was an excellent public speaker. Probably the best I knew. And, apparently, the best Sister Steenblick knew as well.

"No," I said. "Go ahead. Let yourself brag. You ought to take it in stride by now. You ought to know how good you are."

"Yes," he said. "I guess that's easy enough for you to say."

"What do you mean?"

"I guess there aren't too many things that amaze you. Or that impress you."

"I get it," I said. "I'm from New York."

"Yes. But not to look at you."

I sat back and watched a radiator repair shop and a warehouse pass by the window.

"Frankie, by golly, people from New York know how to dress. A matter of hours ago, you were among people who take more pride and care in the way they look than people probably do in Paris or in any other city in the world. The most elegantly dressed women and men on the face of the earth are your neighbors. And here you sit. I tell you, Frankie, if I lived there, I'd spend my last red cent to make dead certain that I was just as elegantly dressed as they are. But here you sit. From New York. In an outfit like that. You have to forgive me if I find it just a little inconceivable."

"The China Doll is just a diner, Dad."

"My last red cent," he reiterated.

A truck was ahead of us, an ancient, slow-moving flatbed with one of its mudflaps gone. It carried a cargo of welding tanks that a rusted and swaying length of chain, slung across the side gates, held upright against the back of the cab. It was doing maybe half the speed limit if it was moving at all.

"When I remember New York, Frankie, I remember all the usual things you'd expect an old timer like me to remember. The Statue of Liberty. There isn't a statue in the world, Frankie, that means as much to me as that statue does. And the Brooklyn Bridge. Do you know that the Brooklyn Bridge was designed by a Swiss architect? No, I might be wrong, he might have been an engineer. But he was Swiss, Frankie. Think of that. I think his name was Roebling. He was from the old country. Just like you. By golly, Frankie, I envy you, living where you can see those sights any time you'd like to. But you don't seem to care. You don't seem to realize that living there is a responsibility as much as it is a privilege, and that this responsibility is to show some respect for what that great city represents. To show by your appearance how proud you are to live there. What I really find inconceivable is that you can walk down the street and not see the difference between yourself and how other people on the street are dressed. I don't mean the bums or the people without homes to go to. You know who I mean."

"You should know," I said, "that there are a lot of people who live there who don't work that hard at dressing right."

"Dressing right," my father retorted, "is not hard work."

As though he'd just now noticed the truck he'd been following at a distance of about two feet, as though he'd just now realized we'd been crawling along at about twenty miles an hour, my father, angrily, suddenly shifted down, yanked the Rabbit into the passing lane, accelerated past the truck, and swung back severely into the lane in front of it.

"All right," I said. "It isn't hard work. I didn't mean that. All I meant to say was that the people you're talking about either don't go around like that all the time or pretty much constitute a minority if they do."

He began laughing.

"By golly, Frankie," he said, "there's something else that I find inconceivable. That you can sit here and tell me something as false and preposterous as that with an absolutely sober face."

"It happens to be the truth."

"What do you know, Frankie, about the truth."

"Enough to get by on."

"Truth, Frankie, is not gasoline."

"Whatever it is, Dad, it still seems to be the one thing you and I don't have any business talking about."

"No, Frankie," he said. "It's the one thing you and I have to still agree on. Look. Look over there."

He waved an arm across the car at my side of Redwood Road. We still had a few blocks to go to the China Doll. Out my window were the usual outskirts buildings, indecorous, utilitarian, blockish, low in profile, buildings inside which items like missile guidance systems, computer circuitboards, and incredibly high-speed cameras for use in surveillance aircraft were manufactured. I'd worked in some of them. I'd put myself through college punching their clocks on the graveyard shift. I wondered, now, why he'd waved at them so grandly.

"I can stop the car right now," he said. "We can go into the lobby of any one of these buildings. Take your pick. We'll pick up a magazine in the waiting room and I'll find an advertisement that will make it clear to you how men and women in New York dress. I'm aware of the fact that an advertisement is poor evidence. But it's all the evidence I have at hand at the moment."

"Listen, Dad," I said. "Come to New York. We'll walk around. We'll talk. We'll spend some time seeing the sights. Maybe you'll want to come and hear the band."

"I've been to New York, Frankie."

"I know you have. And that was thirty years ago. We had just arrived on the ship. And we got there at night. You were wearing that tie you'd bought on the ship. It had an American flag on it. There was a red carnation in your lapel. You were out there on the observation deck, at night in the rain, ready to pay your regards to the Statue of Liberty. But you couldn't see her in the rain and the dark. You used to complain to us about that. And then we took a cab from the dock straight out across Manhattan to the airport. You must have been in New York all of twenty minutes. All that you could really have seen were the lights. There's no way in hell you could have seen many people. You couldn't have seen much more than the theater crowd."

My father laughed again. By now I recognized the laugh as his deliberate sign, a sign not without its warped and minor sense of victory, that I'd just succeeded at making myself inconceivable by another few degrees. I stared bitterly down the road. What I found inconceivable was that we were arguing about New York.

"You were four years old, Frankie. You were in the back seat. You were asleep with your head in Mother's lap. I remember that as clearly as my name. When we got to Idlewild, she handed you to me, and I carried you through the airport until we found the flight for Chicago. You didn't wake up until I buckled your seatbelt. And now you presume to tell me what I saw. No, Frankie, I'm afraid you'll have to admit that it was you who didn't see New York."

"Right," I said. "I guess it doesn't count that I see it now. That I see it every day. That what I see on the street are men and women who've spent their last red cent on a lavender Stetson or a pair of cowboy boots made of something like turkey skin. That what I see are these sad-eyed kids from the projects who've spent their last red cent buying the right pair of hundred-dollar Nikes. That what I see are receptionists who can't afford to live within forty miles of the midtown office where they work but feel compelled to shell out over two hundred bucks for the designer sunglasses that happen to be hip that week. You know why? Because there are people in high and powerful positions who, like you, tell people what to wear. They make a killing off project kids and receptionists from Newark. You know what a jacket like mine goes for? With spots like this worn into the leather at the factory? Two hundred and up. And they're not even your own spots. You see stockbrokers wearing them on the weekends and you'd think they'd spent the last ten years on their backs in the dirt, getting thrown off horses, or on a garage floor, building a stock car."

"The eye of the beholder."

"That's a dirty crack."

"If I lived there I would show you otherwise."

"If you lived there, Dad, you'd have to go around with a bag over your head to preserve your opinions of the place."

"Obviously, Frankie, that is what you do."

I sank back against the headrest. Where, I started wondering, where in New York would my father live or go and find it possible to sustain this picture of the way its population dressed? On what avenue or street would he find exclusively the kind of men dressed in Burberrys trenchcoats, Calvin Klein or Saint Laurie suits, and Hermes ties? On which promenade would he locate this uninterrupted procession of women attired in Gianni Versace knickers and shirt-sleeve jackets or Givenchy blouses, Frances Henaghan wrap dresses, Emilio Gucci furs, or Elizabeth Arden kimonos? How indestructible was his concern with clothes? Why was his own suit pink? Why was he wearing it now? To please me? Faced with the persevering truth of these outskirts in which I knew he had to work, faced with the uncompromising and hangdog panorama of these radiator shops, these warehouses, these discount tire outlets, why for the love of God was he wearing a pink suit? Why did he bother to match a shirt and a tie to it? Why did he bother to shine his shoes to such a gloss? Who did he imagine cared?

I was sitting next to him, strapped into a Volkswagen Rabbit, as a passenger, under the kind of sunlight that did not allow for illusion. And yet it came to me effortlessly to imagine my father walking, at that moment, through New York.

I saw him walking up Park in the direction of Grand Central. When he got to the corner of 40th I saw him stop. A new highrise was going up across the intersection. He'd stopped, as I'd done on occasion, to marvel at the high and improbable cantilever of the crane rising from the most recently poured floor. He was dressed pretty much the way he was now, in a pink suit, and the triumphant smile I'd heard just now in his voice, indicating that he'd netted another of my inconceivabilities, was on his face. I added a Bill Blass raincoat and put a collapsible tweed hat on his head. I put a Conrail commuter pass for a New Haven train into his pocket. At first, I didn't understand why he'd be carrying the pass, but then I saw why. I'd brought New York to a standstill. I'd evacuated New York of all but the well-heeled fraction of its population.

Across the intersection the highrise my father was watching looked as if a bomb scare had emptied it. The crane was idle. The clothes worn by construction workers hadn't fit the picture my father insisted on, and so the workers were gone, gone along with anyone else who couldn't be taken off the street and placed immediately into some advertisement for clothes. There wasn't a cab in sight. Some woman in a fur coat, deprived of her maid, was walking her Yorkie across the street. Bobby Short, I realized, was the only musician left in town. To restore New York to its eclectic character, to its famous wayward clamor of motion and noise, to its sneaker-shod population of secretaries, my father would have to leave. I couldn't keep him there for long. I saw him drop the angle of his profile from the crane, look quickly at his wrist, and frown. Until I saw him push back the cuff of his raincoat, I hadn't known that I'd put a Rolex Perpetual Oyster on his wrist. He straightened his cuff, looked to see if the light was in his favor, and hurried across 40th Street to his train.

"You just missed the China Doll," I said.

"I know. I'm sorry, Frankie, but I just can't take you there. Not the way you're dressed."

"You're joking."

"I'm joking? You come from New York like that and I'm the one who's joking? Dire Straits. Now that's what I call joking."

"So where are we going."

"I don't know, Frankie. I just don't know."

"We can't just drive around for an hour, Dad. Why don't we go look for an empty park and talk about something other than how I'm dressed."

"I'd be disappointed in myself. I ought to do something more for you than that."

After my mother's funeral, I'd returned to New York before my father had picked out the headstone, before my mother's headstone came to occupy half the plot my father had bought at the cemetery. I'd flown back home, I recalled, to a memory of my mother resting underneath this incongruously heavy blanket of soil and a lighter comforter of lilies, daffodils and roses, wishing the weather had been colder so that I wouldn't have had to see them begin to wilt. My father had written a meticulous description of the headstone in one of his letters. I recalled that at the time he wrote he hadn't dressed out the stone with any scripture. Reading his reason that day, back in the studio, had brought water to my eyes. His reason had been that he'd found a hundred scriptures that had spoken with equal familiarity and truth about my mother, and that choosing one of them had been impossible. The idea of going there now, on this bright Friday on my way to Los Angeles, wasn't the way I'd planned it, but it sounded like a way out of this aimless deadlock in the outskirts.

"You could take me to the cemetery, Dad," I said. "I've never seen the headstone."

I watched his face become immediately reflective. I felt like a thief. I'd just forced him to run for a train.

"I will," he said. "But not in that outfit."

"Then we're at another impasse."

"No, Frankie," he said. "We're not."

He turned the Rabbit off onto another outskirts highway that I knew would take us away from the cemetery. We were driving along in silence again. I had no notion of a destination until he pulled the Rabbit into a shopping mall I hadn't seen before.

"You're going to buy me some clothes," I said.

He was already out of the car.

"Come along," he said. "We don't have much time."

He took off. I hung back long enough to get my trumpet out of the back seat and lock the doors. When I found him, he was talking to a salesman beneath the metal awning of an Endicott-Johnson shoe store. The awning was in homage, I suppose, to a time when stores like this were actually exposed to weather and the shoes displayed in the windows had to be protected from the sunlight. The salesman and my father were standing beside a circular patio table on which shoes had been layered, like the leaves of an artichoke, in tiered and concentric circles. The salesman was young and reminded me of a kind of friend I might have admired for his aptitude for hunting deer with a bow had I gone on living in Salt Lake. I felt as alien as I think I ever have. I felt a desperate loneliness for Jill and her ability to walk away from situations like this as though they were broken umbrellas or abandoned cars. A shoe was in one of the salesman's hands.

"So," my father said, in his jocular way with people to whom he wasn't related. "This is the bum I was telling you about."

"You from New York?" the salesman asked.

"It's where I live."

"See anything here you like?"

I looked at the shoe he was slowly revolving in his hand.

"I'm not wearing socks."

"No problem," he said. "We sell socks."

At the cemetery, I stood and looked at the headstone for what must have been twenty minutes before I said anything. Beneath the stone, beneath the rows of flowers my father had planted directly in front of it, my mother was laid out on her back, the way she'd been at the viewing and the time or two I'd stolen a look into her bedroom during her regular afternoon nap. She was waiting now for what my father called the Morning of the First Resurrection. The shirt I was wearing, white and new enough that it still had these boxlike folds across the front, was scratchy. The Endicott-Johnson wingtips were starting to hurt my feet. The seersucker suit, whose sleeves I'd have a New York tailor shorten, felt weightless, and let the light wind there on the hillside through to my legs. And I couldn't look down at the headstone without seeing the end of my tie, a thin, knitted length of blue wool whose motion in the wind was something I wasn't accustomed to. My father was standing next to me. His smile was broad and involuntary. The strenuous lines I'd seen in his face at the airport had lost the nervous strength that had given them their force. His pride was palpable. He'd kept the grave immaculate.

"It's a beautiful headstone, Dad. Elegant. Simple. It's the one she would have picked herself."

I felt lame and uninventive.

"Do you really think so?" he said.

"Yes. I think she would have wanted it without a scripture."

"You think so too, Frankie? By golly, I can't tell you what a relief it is to hear you say so. I'm going to have to spend a very long time with her, and you know how difficult she could be when I did something that didn't make her happy."

"Remember the piano?" I said.

"Of course." He laughed softly. "The old Boesendorfer. Across the Atlantic. And then the music from the basement. Well, Frankie, if there's a heaven for your mother, then there's a Boesendorfer there, and I'm pretty sure she's found the right house for it by now."

"She might have gotten to where she liked it downstairs. Who knows. After thirty years, I mean. It could have grown on her."

"That's also possible."

What came to my mind right then was the tale I'd heard at the mission home about the mother who had told her son to come home from his mission either pure or in a coffin. I wondered if her son had seen, in his mother's farewell ultimatum, the tyranny and weakness of all those women so witlessly and fanatically determined to make child stars or presidents of their children. I wondered what kind of man he'd turned out to be. A kind man? Brutal? An accountant? A poet? The one thing I knew for certain, there on the hillside, was that my mother would have cringed at a scripture on her headstone.

My father was looking at the grave. "I imagine we'll all be spending some time with her again," I said.

"Yes," he said. "As long as we can hold the family together."

"She might not be as difficult now."

"No." My father shook his head and smiled. "I doubt that very much. Not even the Kingdom of Heaven could change her. Besides, I don't want her changed. I want her exactly the way she was."

"I love you very much," I said. "Come to New York."

He stared at me.

"I've been to New York, Frankie."

"I should be getting back to the airport, Dad."

"Already? Wait. I'll tell you what. Let's forget about going to the China Doll. I'll take you to the Hotel Utah."

"I have to go, Dad. Honest."

At the airport, I got my trumpet and my old clothes, bundled up in a shopping bag, out of the back seat of the Rabbit. I said goodbye to my father at the gate. There, among a casual scattering of mid-afternoon passengers heading for California, I said goodbye to the man who'd left a comprehensible life in Zurich in order to pursue, with his family, the Kingdom of Dreams in as unlikely a place as this. We embraced. I felt again the restless current that defined him as a man and as my father. The channel in which that current ran was indestructible. He would reach the Kingdom dressed to the best of his sartorial knowledge and with his belief in Mormon doctrine untarnished. It was only the current itself, I realized, the flow of that searching and restless river governed by his enormous and sometimes bewildered heart, that ran the risk of being destroyed. An incomprehensible regret had come into his smile again, and had raised the lines of his face to a relief that made him look almost wild. The sockets of his eyes were bright and watery, as I knew mine were, with some perhaps forever unrequited need to have the mystery between us over. I was happy to be in the current of his arms. He watched me board the flight with his hands in his trouser pockets. I hoped, seeing him there, that when I got back home I'd have the vigilance not to turn this moment into some casual anecdote, not to strip it of its fierceness, not to tailor it to the haggard and exhausting levity of a Sunday brunch somewhere; that I'd remember him, back in New York, with Jill, with the crowd at Buck's, with the band, under the influence again of the nervous social appetite of the city in which I lived, not as some exiled, aging prince in a pink suit, but as my father, the one man through whom I could claim any unique and real past, the one man who stood between me and the naked necessity of having to say "I am" to the mirror each morning, loud enough to be distinguished from the wail of the garbage truck in the street outside the window, in order to put recognizable flesh on my face for the rest of the day. I hoped most that he would choose to come to see me soon, and that if he did, the pilot who brought him east to visit me would let him down on New York gently.

ABOUT THE EDITOR Max Zimmer is the author of the Shake Tauffler novels, a coming of age story about a boy growing up Mormon in 50s and 60s Utah with a dream to play jazz trumpet as he searches for meaning while religion and jazz do battle for his soul. He earned a B.A. and M.A. in creative writing from the University of Utah. An invitation to a summer at Yaddo, the writers and artists retreat in upstate New York, brought him east, where he has stayed. He has taught fiction writing at the University of Utah and SUNY Oswego. He works with aspiring writers to bring out their best.

His published work includes poems, stories, reviews, biographies, translations, columns for an automotive magazine, and liner notes for jazz albums. His work has been taught in college courses. Nominated by Raymond Carver, his first published story "Utah Died for your Sins" was awarded the Pushcart Prize. E. L. Doctorow, Jack Cady, Grace Paley, Lewis Turco, and John Gardner are among the writers who have championed his work; John Cheever enthusiastically promoted Max's work for the last five years of his life.